The Legacy of Sterling Manor

JENNIFER FRANZ GRIFFITH

Prologue

January 1, 2018

"If I loved you less, I might be able to talk about it more."

Jane Austen, Emma

It has been nearly sixty-five years since I kept a diary – journaled, as it is called now. I didn't want to talk to anyone, not even myself. I thought if I let out my feelings, they would crush me. So instead, I lived a lifetime in a house, that was not mine, alone with my sorrow. I never let anyone in. Not into my heart and rarely into the house. I was once a young girl full of life and hope for the future until reality crashed into my dream, killing it instantly.

I tried to freeze time to never change anything from when I was the happiest, but time does not freeze. It moves on with or without you. If you do not change with the time, you wither away like the paint on a wall, peeling and cracking and becoming something ugly, something old and broken.

You can be brave and live life to the fullest, overcoming all obstacles, or you can let life wear you down until you are a mere survivor of its cruelness. It is your choice.

Had I the chance to live it again, I would still choose love. But I fear we do not get second chances when time runs out and my time here has come to its end.

Chapter One

*B*e brave, I told myself as I walked the three blocks to the townhouse that I shared with two roommates. I had done this walk of shame more than once – and no, it's not *that* kind of walk of shame. I'd actually have to have a man in my life for that to happen and I haven't for about six months.

My shoulders tightened as I worried about breaking the news to my roommates. They were not understanding friends. Actually, they were not my friends at all – understanding or otherwise. I found the house share ad on Craigslist. Yes, people still use Craigslist to post things like legitimate house share ads – not just lures disguised as ads with the intent to kill you. I had to convince my parents of that fact before they would get off my case about entertaining the idea of answering the ad.

If you met my roommates, the idea of them killing someone would seem ridiculous. For one, they wouldn't have the time. Both were laser-focused on their dream careers, dream lives, and dream husbands. They were both twenty-three and had it all together. Here I was thirty-years-old and couldn't seem to find my path or the bus schedule to get on the right path!

Perry, the beautiful blonde psychology major, whose parents owned the house we lived in was not a nice person – at least not to me. We communicated mostly by Post-it notes on the refrigerator indicating what infraction I had committed the day before.

My other roommate Darla spent hours learning make-up techniques to contour and hide every flaw and even shared them on her YouTube channel mostly as a means to find a rich husband, but she was the friendlier of the two roommates.

When I got to the house, both Perry and Darla were home which was a rare thing, but I could say this to both of them at once. I took my key out and unlocked the front door. Perry was on the sofa studying and Darla was sitting next to her watching something on her phone.

"Oh, hey Holly," Darla said, and then focused back on her phone. Perry looked up from her laptop for a second to barely acknowledge my presence.

"Hey," I said back, "so I should tell you…"

"Oh no, Hol-leeee," Darla said, drawing out my name with a mix of pity and annoyance in her voice. "Did you quit another job just before the rent is due?"

"Yes," I started, "but the job just wasn't right for me."

"They never are," Perry said, dryly, still staring at her computer. Maybe I did this more than I realized if Perry was able to notice a pattern.

"What is that supposed to mean?" I asked, honestly wondering what they thought my problem was.

"These jobs are like drugs to you. You are addicted to job-hopping," Perry analyzed, looking me straight in the eye over her laptop screen.

The sound of her voice was jarring since I heard it so little.

I shook my head quickly with exaggeration that I didn't agree with her ridiculous diagnosis. "I'm not addicted to job-hopping," I replied. I hoped she had to take some kind of practical test before she was allowed to spew this nonsense on to actual clients. "Look, maybe I'm not as driven as the two of you. I haven't known my whole life what I was meant to do. I'm still trying to figure stuff out." I added that last part hoping that Perry would back off if I spouted off some random psychobabble that I picked up from the movies.

"Girl, you're thirty. You do not have much time left. Soon your looks are going to go – although if you'd let me give you some makeup tips it could help." Darla interjected. Perry gave her a side-eye. "I'm just saying you better find yourself already. The clock is ticking, and you are going to end up as a bitter old lady who lives all alone."

Rubbing my eyes in exasperation, I walked out of the living room and up the stairs to my bedroom – my sanctuary. Opening the door to the room, I took a deep breath and inhaled the smell of my vanilla body lotion still lingering in the air from this morning. I headed straight to my bed. It was a twin that fit well in the small room and was pushed up against the corner of two walls. The mattress was topped with gel foam, covered by 500 thread count dark pink sheets I splurged on after one of my better paydays. I had fluffy pillows and an ombré pink puffy duvet to top it all off. Beyond my fancy bed accessories, there was not much else in the room. It was all I needed – a comfortable place to sleep and to think.

I reflected on what my two housemates had said to me. Maybe I did go through jobs like Darla went through men. Maybe I should have said that to her instead of just standing there and taking it. And maybe I could have mentioned the pills that Perry took to keep herself going. I was not the type of person to stoop to such pettiness. Despite my apparent flightiness, I had a good head on my shoulders and maturity beyond my years as my grandma had liked to say. Okay, maybe she was wrong, and I hadn't figured out what it meant be a mature adult yet.

I graduated from college with a BA in business determined to be a successful entrepreneur and I wanted to work hard to build my business from the ground up. The only problem was I didn't have a clear vision of what that business would be.

My father suggested that I try a few jobs to see what fit. So, I did. I started at a restaurant thinking that maybe owning a restaurant was what I wanted to do. A childhood friend's family owned The Bistro Italiano and I worked there starting with bussing tables all the way to waitress and from there to line cook. From this experience, I discovered my love of cooking. I also realized that running a restaurant came with a lifestyle that I had no interest in.

Next, I took a job as a concierge at a hotel in the city. I thought that perhaps the hospitality industry had a place for me. I loved taking reservations and helping guests who appreciated the extra mile you would go for them. I even liked appeasing the troubled guest and turning a complaint into a compliment. I learned that if you didn't manage a hotel properly then your staff would rise against you, especially if you made them do things that weren't in their job descriptions like cleaning rooms and shoveling snow. I was part of a mass exodus from that hotel. Some of my co-workers who quit at the same time I did threatened to sue the hotel for mismanagement.

After that was another series of other failed attempts. I worked at a bakery where I learned that I was good at making desserts, but I hated getting up for work so early. I worked as an apprentice to an interior designer. I did marketing and maintained the social media pages of a small boutique. I worked in a childcare center, as a barista at a coffee bar, and the latest job I left today as a dog groomer – allergic to dogs.

Why couldn't I find what I was supposed to do? Maybe even more of a problem was that in all the jobs I tried, I never made any lasting friendships. I hadn't found my tribe. I flopped over, burying myself in one of my enormous pillows when my cell phone rang.

"Hello," I answered, hoping it was not a telemarketer. Even I didn't want to do that job.

"Hello. Is this Holly Jensen?" a male voice on the other end of the phone asked.

Great. It was a telemarketer. "Listen, let me save you from your scripted speech. I don't have any money to buy whatever you are selling."

I was about to hang up, when I heard the voice say, "No, no, please wait. I am Randall Sullivan, legal counsel for Celia Anderson's estate in Friendsville. She was your aunt."

Give me a break, I thought. These people and their scams. Next, he would ask for my bank account and social security number. "Thank you but I'm not interested," I said and hung up.

The phone rang again with the same number. I thought it was odd. Usually, they didn't call you back once you said you were not interested. I decided to call my mother.

I found her number in my recents list and pressed call. She answered on the third ring.

"Mom, do I have an Aunt Celia?" I asked without saying hello first. She hated when I did that. I could imagine her face all scrunched up in disapproval.

I looked a lot like my mom. Like the rest of the women on her side of the family, we both had the same red hair, green eyes, thin frames, and pale skin. I probably even made that same scrunched up face of disapproval. She was petite where I was tall though. I must have gotten that from my dad's side.

"Well hello to you too," she said with the sarcastic response I was expecting. "Yes, you do have an Aunt Celia. She is my mother's sister. So, she would be your great-aunt. I think you might have only met her once when you were little. We've never had much contact with her. Why?"

"I think she died," I answered quietly.

"That's odd. I would have thought your Grandma Alice would have come to me with that information," she said. The thing that is odd about that statement is that my Grandma Alice has been dead for ten years and my mother believes she can still make contact with her spirit.

Letting that craziness go, I told my mother about the phone call I received from some man who said he was her lawyer. I told her that he said she lived in someplace called Friendsville. She confirmed that was correct. Aunt Celia had lived in Friendsville and we had even visited her there once, years ago, with my Grandma Alice before she died.

After getting off the phone with my mother, making sure to say a proper goodbye, I decided to call back the lawyer's number from the caller ID in my phone. I Googled it first though, to make sure it was a legitimate number. According to Google, the number did belong to Randall F. Sullivan, Esq.

"Hello, Ms. Jensen?" he asked already knowing the answer. "I'm so glad you called back."

Mr. Sullivan went on to explain that my great-aunt died about a month ago. There wasn't a funeral to speak of. He was instructed that at the time of her death to have her body cremated and her ashes spread in the ocean. He had already taken care of all of that. He apologized for not contacting me sooner, but he was not aware that she had any family left until he came across my name in the will.

"I didn't know her," I explained still feeling a little sad for her that she had no one at her funeral or whatever spreading someone's ashes constituted, except for a lawyer she paid to be there.

"Huh," he said, sounding puzzled. "Well, she left you a substantial share of her estate."

I wasn't sure what to say. This was only something that happened in books and movies, wasn't it – a long-lost relative leaves you a fortune? I wasn't sure how to ask the next obvious question that was on my mind without sounding like a cold-hearted gold digger.

"I'm not able to tell you the details of your inheritance over the phone," he said, reading my mind and saving me from the awkward question. "You will need to come here to Friendsville to meet me."

I was a little uncomfortable going to a town I was not familiar with to meet a man I didn't know about an inheritance from an aunt I didn't remember. He was kind and understood my trepidation. He suggested that we meet in a public place – a local diner called Dotty's. Still hesitant, I agreed. He gave me directions to the town which was about three hours away. We planned to meet the following day at 9:00 a.m.

Be brave, I told myself for the second time today. Maybe this was a new beginning. Still holding onto that idea, I walked back downstairs to look for Perry and Darla. I found them on the couch exactly where I left them.

I clenched my fists at my sides and blurted, "I am moving out – effective tomorrow."

"Okay," Darla answered, making duck lips at her phone and tracing over her cheeks with an invisible makeup brush.

I wasn't sure what kind of reaction to my news I expected. Some reaction would have been nice. "I will send you the money for the rent this month," I added quickly, not sure where I was going to get it from.

"Forget it," Perry said as she started typing furiously on her laptop. She was probably reposting the "roommate wanted" ad back on Craigslist already.

I let out the breath I didn't realize I was holding and walked back up to my room to start packing. I would have to get an early start if I had any hope of getting there on time for my meeting.

It didn't matter if this inheritance turned out to be a windfall or a bust. My new beginning was going to start by finding a place to live where people cared about me.

Chapter Two

*T*he next day I packed up all my worldly possessions in my car. Convenient though it was, I was little off put by the fact that everything I owned fit into my Ford Focus. All the furniture in the apartment was there when I moved in. Even the bed was not mine. It was left there by a previous roommate who married and upgraded to a king-size bed with her husband. She called it her contribution to the apartment. It was probably out of guilt for leaving three months before the apartment lease was up. Not that I had any room to judge. I thought that bed might bring me some luck in the romance department. It had not.

I stopped at the local convenience store before starting my three-hour journey. I grabbed three bottles of water and some trail mix. Stuffing my face with chips and cookies was something I would typically do, but this time was going to be different from the start.

Getting back in my car, I took a deep breath, reminding myself that whatever Friendsville had in store for me was more than I had now —

even if the inheritance was ten bucks or a lonely goat. I would make lemonade out of lemons and find my place in the world.

Okay, enough with the self-motivating inner dialogue. It was time to go. As the Bluetooth in my phone paired with my car's speakers, I put on my pumped-up playlist consisting of Katy Perry, Sia and Beyonce and started singing at the top of my lungs. I was ready for whatever was waiting for me.

What was waiting for me, I discovered 190 miles later, was the smallest town I had ever seen. I was sure that if I blinked, I would have missed it.

I stopped in front of a large faded sign that greeted me at the edge of the town. It read, "Welcome to Friendsville. Population 489" in blue script lettering. Population 489? My high school graduating class was nearly the size of the entire population of this town.

I continued driving slowly with my eyes wide to take in everything. Past the sign was a VFW hall advertising a "Spring Fling" promising music, dinner, and dancing on Saturday night. Beyond the hall were a few buildings that looked abandoned and then a long, straight bridge – long being comparative to the size of the town. Peering over the bridge, I saw a breathtaking view of a wide-mouthed river – calm waters near the bridge, white water farther out. The banks of the river were lined with tall trees just starting to fill in the scene with their green leaves. I imaged how majestic autumn with the changing colors of the leaves must have made this place look. Clearly this was the town's claim to fame if there was one.

Moving across the bridge, I saw more buildings that appeared abandoned and then I passed what I thought was a house, but according to the sign was McFarland's Market. Across the street from the market was a gas station. Then there was a pub with what looked like a hand-painted sign hanging off the side of it. I couldn't make out the name of it, but I made a note of its location because I had a feeling, I might need to have a drink before this day was through.

Then there was a laundromat, a sub shop, a cell phone store, the library, and a natural foods store lining each side of what I discovered was Main Street. I wondered if it was not just the main street, but the only street in the whole town. I pulled over into a parking spot on the street. Looking farther down Main Street, I could see a church and across from that a doctor's office with a pharmacy attached. I couldn't make out any specific businesses past that from my vantage point, but it seemed there was more to town farther down the road.

I opened my glove compartment to find the paper where I wrote down the name of the place Mr. Sullivan told me to meet him. It was called Dotty's Diner. I realized after looking around that I was parked right in front of it. I was also sure that it was the only diner in this town.

Before getting out of my car, I texted my mother.

Me: Arrived safety in Friendsville.

Mom: Be safe and let me know what happens.

It was 9:06 a.m. by that time and I was late for my meeting. I looked to see if there was a meter or a sign telling me not to park there. All I needed was a ticket or my car to get towed. I mean that was how my luck was running these days. There wasn't a sign or a meter or a painted curb anywhere in sight. Maybe I was going to catch a break today.

I opened the door to the diner causing the bell hooked to the top to ring. It felt like everyone inside stopped to look at me. I guess this was not exactly a tourist attraction. I figured that everyone was sizing me up, wondering what my business was there. I tried to ignore the stares and was relieved to be welcomed by Dotty herself, or so her name tag claimed.

"Well hello there darling. Welcome. Grab a seat wherever you like," Dotty instructed as she poured coffee for the people at the table closest to the door.

Now it was my turn to size up the place to try and find Mr. Sullivan. It turned out that I didn't have to look too hard. An older man with graying hair and a matching moustache waved me over to his table. Assuming he must have figured out who I was as the only person he didn't know in the diner, I walked over to his table.

"Mr. Sullivan?" I asked timidly, trying not to draw any more attention to myself. Meeting with a lawyer in a town this small was likely cause for gossip as it was, and I really didn't like people knowing my business. Clearly, if I was going to stay here for more than five minutes, I was going to have to get over that.

"Yes, Holly. Please come and sit," he directed. "Dotty, some coffee over here when you get a chance, please?" He winked at her as he asked, and she nodded bringing over her coffee pot immediately.

"Holly, is it?" Dotty asked as she turned over my cup and poured the coffee in. She must have overheard him say my name. I nodded. This was absolutely an everybody-knows-everybody's-business type of town. "Well, welcome to Friendsville, darling. You were Ms. Celia's niece, right? I'm so sorry for your loss." She seemed genuine and gave my shoulder a tiny squeeze as she moved onto the next table with her coffee pot. Well, maybe it was not all bad if people knew things about you. I didn't feel compelled to tell her that my aunt Celia was basically a stranger to me. At that moment, it really occurred to me that I had no idea what I was doing here.

I turned to Mr. Sullivan, watching as he added three packets of sugar to his coffee and a hefty amount of cream. "Mr. Sullivan, I'm not really sure why Aunt Celia would leave anything to me. I barely knew her. I think I visited her with my mother and my grandmother once when I was six."

"That must have been some memorable visit then," he said smiling as he put his coffee down to rifle through his briefcase.

"Honestly, I had to call my mother to ask if I even had an Aunt Celia. She is the one who reminded me that I came here once. I vaguely remembered the visit after she mentioned it. Thinking about it, all I remember is being afraid of this strange woman people were telling me was my aunt," I said trying to recollect anything that might have happened that day.

"Most people were scared of her to tell you the truth," he said matter-of-factly. He found what he was looking for in his briefcase, cleared his throat and began. "This is a letter from your aunt addressed to you, but I have been instructed to read it aloud to you."

Well, that seemed weird, but whatever. I nodded for him to continue.

Clearing his throat again, he began to read the letter. "Dear Holly. I am sure that you hardly remember me. After the passing of your grandmother – my sister Alice, the family didn't have much to do with me. I can't blame them. I was a nasty, bitter old lady. Who would want to spend more time than they had to with someone like that? For many years I drove people away. Your grandmother forced your mother to visit with me even though I know she dreaded every minute of it. Then there was that time when you came along with them. You were a sweet little six-year-old angel in your white smocked dress and your darling red hair in pigtails. While your grandmother and mother busied themselves in the kitchen preparing lunch, I sat in that same chair I always sat in – annoyed that people were in my house upsetting my routine. You somehow managed to climb into my lap without me even moving to let you in. "Auntie Celia, why do you look so sad? Please smile for me," you said. How could I not smile? Then you said, and I never forgot, "You have the most beautiful smile I've ever seen!" You proceeded to curl up closer to me and fell asleep. It was the most peace I had felt in a century. That moment meant the world to me. So, to you I give my whole world."

After finishing the letter, Mr. Sullivan and I sat silently for a few minutes. I thought about that day. My parents have a picture on their living room wall of me as a little girl, wearing that white smocked dress with my hair in pigtails. I am sure I wore that dress more than once and I always had my hair in pigtails, but what if that picture was taken on this day my aunt spoke of? If it were not for the photo, I would have questioned if she had the right child. I racked my brain to come up with a clearer memory of that day. I could see my mother, grandmother and I walking up to a beautiful house and when we got inside there was a woman sitting on a stiff high-back chair. She probably would have been about 56 or 57 years old at the time, but she looked much older than that. She had a scowl on her face, and I was afraid of her. I don't remember climbing into her lap or even talking to her. That is something that a brave person would do. I struggle with having courage to do things now, at thirty, I doubted that I was ever that brave as a child.

"Holly?" Mr. Sullivan spoke and interrupted my thoughts. I looked over at him, not quite ready to know what her whole world was yet that she was gifting to me.

"Mr. Sullivan? Did you know my aunt well?" I asked, wanting to know more about this person who thought so highly of me, but I knew basically nothing about.

Mr. Sullivan shifted and rubbed his chin. He looked like he was trying to choose his words carefully. "I was your aunt's lawyer for the last twenty years." He stopped, clearly wondering if that would be enough for me. It wasn't.

Smiling, I prodded on. "What was she like?"

"She…" he trailed off, once again looking for the right words. "She was one of the town elders. She went to church every Sunday and sat in the same seat. She drove her car into town to grocery shop every Wednesday morning. Beyond that she mostly kept to herself in her house."

"Yes, but what was she like?" I asked again not letting him off the hook. "And you don't need to sugar-coat it if that's what you are worried about."

Mr. Sullivan sighed. "I don't really know. Listen, I don't want to speak ill of the dead, but she didn't seem like a very nice lady. I don't mean that she went around slashing people's tires or chasing children off her porch with a broom or anything. She just was not the type who liked people. When Celia came into town, people moved out of her way just because of the look on her face – that annoyed look she mentioned in her letter. She never smiled. When I came to her house the few times she needed me for legal questions, not big things, just things like her will, she was very proper, offered me tea and then was all business. It was like she didn't want to waste her words."

I sat there for a moment, feeling sad. She was all alone, but I suppose she liked it that way. My family never spoke about her. I don't think that she ever married and certainly didn't have any children, or I doubt that I would be sitting here today waiting to find out what my inheritance was.

"I'm sorry if I upset you. She may have had friends in town. I mean I was just her lawyer. I wasn't that close to her," he backpedaled like he wanted to take the sting out of what he said.

17

"No, no. It's okay. I wanted to know. Thank you for being honest." I responded. Now I was trying to make him feel better.

Mr. Sullivan reached into his briefcase again and pulled out some documents. "Speaking of getting down to business, would you like to know what she left you in her will?"

I nodded.

"She left you her house, everything in it and two hundred thousand dollars," he announced, smiling, and waiting for my reaction.

I was speechless.

Mr. Sullivan sat there for a while, letting the significance of what he just told me sink in. Before I could even process the gift that I had just received, someone burst through the door of the diner. The door opened so forcefully that it sounded like that bell was going to come right off its hinges.

I barely had time to take in what the person looked like before he came charging at our table.

"Randy, that house belongs to my family! It was purchased by my grandfather, Graham Sterling, and it should rightfully be turned over to me." the man shouted.

Mr. Sullivan looked mortified, but not shocked by the man's outburst. This seemed like an issue he was already familiar with. I, on the other hand, sat wide-eyed and said nothing. It didn't seem like it should be any of my business. Unfortunately, now it was.

"Derek," Mr. Sullivan addressed the shouting man, "this really isn't the time."

Unwavering, the man continued with his tirade. "This is absolutely the time. The estate is going to someone who I am sure is not part of my family even though my grandfather bought that house and that woman squatted in it for seventy years."

He was so focused on proving his point, I'm not sure he even realized that there was another person sitting at the table. I noticed him though. He was maybe just a few years older than me. Dressed in a blue suit with a burgundy satin tie, he looked like he just stepped out of a corporate board meeting which seemed out of place for someone who was from this little Podunk town. There were a few tells that I noticed that didn't fit this professional look he seemed to be going for. The first thing was he needed a haircut. His dark blond hair just brushed the top of his collar and swept slightly across his brow. He was not unkempt, but a man in a power suit wouldn't have let something as important as the length of his hair go unchecked. The second thing I noticed were his socks. They were burgundy like his tie, but they had cows on them. What I was trying not to notice was how handsome he was – even with his reddening face and furrowed brow, looking at him made my heart race a little.

"Holly," Mr. Sullivan said, bringing my attention back to the table. "Let me apologize for our town council president's irrational behavior."

The councilman stopped after being called out in his professional title and looked at me like he had indeed just noticed that I was sitting there. His face reddened again, but this time it was more of a blush.

"This is Derek Sterling. He is the president of our town council and believe it or not he is actually a beloved member of this community," Mr. Sullivan said speaking only to me.

"I'm so sorry. You must think I am an idiot – a very loud idiot," Derek apologized, flashing me a smile that made that heart racing thing happen again. This time it was my turn to blush.

"Derek, this is Holly Jensen, Celia Anderson's great niece," Mr. Sullivan stated, folded his arms, and sat back in his chair with a smirk.

Derek's smile faded and his face blanched. At that moment, I realized the house in question was my house, well Aunt Celia's house. It seemed that I was not only inheriting a house today, I was also inheriting an age-old feud.

"It's nice to meet you," I said innocently, extending my hand to him.

Maybe I was imaging it, but the entire diner was frozen but for the few whispers and murmurs. It was Dotty who broke the tension. She came up behind Derek, slightly pushing him to sit in the chair behind him and when he did, she flipped over his cup and poured him some coffee. I guess coffee fixed everything in this town.

"Holly," Dotty said addressing me. "Derek's family has been part of this town for seventy-five years. His grandfather was the town's sheriff and now Derek has become our town's champion with his policies and plans for expanding the town. I don't know if you noticed, but this town is not exactly thriving, but Derek has plans to put us on the map. Don't ya, darling?"

It was like she needed to fill the space in the room with her words. I had no idea why she was telling me this. Did she want me to know that he was really a great guy? Was she on his side in this feud? From what I had heard about Celia, I was not sure that anyone could possibly be on her side or even if she would have let them.

Derek finally spoke. "I'm sorry to tell you this but your aunt was an illegal tenant of that house. So, if you are here because you think it's yours you are sadly mistaken." He started to get louder with each word. "You would probably be better off leaving now and handing over what is my family's legacy. That would be the right thing to do."

"Oh, horse shit!" Mr. Sullivan exclaimed out of nowhere, slamming his hand on the table, making me jump in my seat. "Your family's legacy my ass. Prove it. Do you have the deed to that house?"

I had to stifle a giggle after Randy's unexpected outburst. After that he was just Randy. We had clearly done away with the formalities.

"Do you?" Derek threw back at him. With that he rose from his chair and started to walk out of the diner, but not before saying to me, "Save yourself some hassle and just walk away from this house." Then he was out the door with the same hurried rage he came in with.

"Okay then," Randy said after letting out a deep breath. "Ready to see the house?"

Chapter Three

I got back in my car and followed Randy as he led me to Celia's house. We drove past the church I saw from my parking spot and turned right on to Maple Street. The house was on the corner and immediately came into view when we turned. As we got closer to the house, I had a strong feeling of déjà vu. Foggy images swirled in my head, but they were unfamiliar, almost like they were someone else's memories entering my mind. I tried to shake off the feeling as we pulled into the long driveway that ended at a detached garage.

The enormous white house was framed with black shutters and doors and was tucked behind a majestic oak tree in the front yard. The lawn was perfectly manicured and followed the sidewalks from two streets that formed a point about a hundred feet from the front door. The roof was steepled in four levels with a set of windows on each. The most stunning of its features was the wrap-around porch that rounded the house completely from each side to the back. I followed along the porch to explore more of the house's exterior. On one side was a brick chimney. At the back of the house was a large fishpond almost like a moat guarding that side of the house. It was lined with large stones and a stone pathway to a garden with a bench where you could sit and watch the fish. It was the most beautiful house I had ever seen and now it was mine.

Randy was already waiting on the porch when I finally finished canvassing the outside of the house. He saw me and dangled keys on what turned out to be a plastic Randall Sullivan, Esq. keychain. I had a feeling I might need his legal services in the future so I thought I should hold on to it just in case.

"Ready to see inside?" he asked with a smile.

I smiled back, took the keys from him, and unlocked the front door. Stepping inside I felt like I was taken back in time to the 1940s. It didn't look like Celia had changed anything since she moved into the house nearly seventy years ago. The house was as beautiful and timeless on the inside as it was on the outside. It was bright and sunny with all the natural light coming in through the windows. The doorway opened to the living room which expanded to the entire front of the house. Some of the walls were painted a bold navy blue while others were covered in wallpaper with the same navy background but with a floral pattern running through it. The furniture was all cherry wood except for two red sofas and loud floral wing-backed chairs that sat facing each other in front of the brick fireplace. The drapes on the windows were red and barely brushed the green patterned wall-to-wall carpet on the floor. On the back wall was an enormous staircase with wooden spindles painted white and carpeted stairs. There was a doorway that led to a narrow kitchen. I couldn't wait to step farther in to explore the rest.

Lost in the beauty of the house, I nearly forgot that Randy was with me until he stepped through the doorway behind me and the floorboard creaked beneath his feet. I turned to look at him and when I turned back it was all gone. The house was not the shining beacon of a bright future as I had seen when I walked through the door. It was dingy at best. All the furniture was covered with bedsheets. The rug was dirty and tattered from years of use. The paint and paper on the walls were peeling and the floors were creaky. The windows that I once saw letting in the light were drafty and cracking around the woodwork.

"I had Celia's housekeeper come in and cover the furniture and clean the place last week," Randy said. I looked at him with confusion. "You okay dear?" he asked me.

Shaking it off I answered, "It was the strangest thing. When I stepped inside, I saw the house differently." I couldn't explain to him what I thought I saw.

"Oh, well maybe you were remembering the time you were here," he offered and then with a bright smile added, "Or maybe you see the potential in this house?"

Of course, he was right. It was probably a mix of both of those things. It was not like I had gone back in time.

"So, what do I do now?" I asked Randy. "Can I stay here? I mean maybe even just for the night?" I thought about driving home to my parents' house and I just didn't want to. I already felt as though I belonged right here.

"Oh yes, the house is yours now. I mean technically. There is some legal work to be done and papers to sign, but we can do that tomorrow," he reassured me.

My house. Mine.

Randy took me for a full tour of the inside of the house. We started with the galley kitchen, barely wide enough for both of us to fit. It wrapped around to the back of the house and led into a large dining room with a heavy cherry wood dining table and chairs in the center with a large china cabinet against the wall. Instead of china, it was filled with trinkets and figurines. Walking through the dining room, we ended back in the living room where the fireplace was. Finishing that floor, we walked up the massive staircase to the second floor. There were five bedrooms and two bathrooms. I cracked open each of the doors to take a quick peek then decided to explore them more later, on my own. Randy showed me the pull-down that led to the attic which was in the middle of the hallway.

He explained that the housekeeper had also changed all the sheets and cleaned everything. He showed me which bedroom had been Celia's. I felt a twinge of anxiety about it. Even though Celia had been in the hospital when she died and hadn't died in the house, I still thought of her room as sacred and chose one of the other bedrooms to drop my bag in.

After the tour, Randy told me more about places in town where I could get anything I needed. There were a grocery store and a pharmacy and a hardware store. For anything complicated, I would have to travel about an hour to the nearest "big city" as he put it, but Amazon did deliver here.

I laughed at that. "Thank you, but I'm not sure if I am going to become a permanent resident."

Randy looked down and rubbed his chin. "Well, that is up to you I guess, but you know what we could use in this town?" he asked, looking up, "A bed and breakfast." With that, he left the porch and waved goodbye as he got into his car.

A bed and breakfast? The house was certainly big enough. It had five bedrooms after all and an enormous living area. I had already envisioned what it would look like. Hadn't I? Maybe a B&B was the perfect thing to tie all my randomly acquired skills together. I worked the hotel job and learned all the ins and outs of the hospitality business. I had worked both as a cook and a baker. I had the bed and the breakfast part down, plus I had a college degree in business. My quest to be an entrepreneur had led me here with all the skills I needed to make it a reality. All of those jobs were stepping stones to my true future. Take that Perry and Darla! I can be brave and make a go of this. I already had a glimpse of what this house could be, and I could restore it and return it to its former glory. I started picturing guests sitting in the living room cozying up to the fireplace and me in a beautiful kitchen creating a magnificent breakfast that they would rave over. That feeling of belonging here was washing over me again.

My daydream was interrupted by the annoying sound of a car horn blaring close by.

It was coming from a black Toyota Tacoma that screeched to a halt in front of the house. The driver barely stopped before jumping out of the truck and walking up the front lawn to where I was standing on the porch. The sun was in my eyes, but it didn't take me long to realize it was Derek Sterling coming by for a not-so-friendly visit. I could tell by the way he was stomping toward me much like the way he had entered the diner. Was this his angry walk or just his walk? Or was he just always angry?

"Mr. Sterling, it's lovely to see you again so soon," I sarcastically shouted as he approached me.

He scowled as he reached the porch, but his expression softened the closer he got. He paused about ten feet from the house for a few seconds or maybe longer. It felt like time shifted somehow and the edges of the world around us were blurred. He looked at me like this was the first time he actually *saw* me. I felt myself squirm as he studied me.

Then I shifted my stance and looked him in the eye as I prepared to literally stand my ground. For just a moment though, I paused to take in the sight of him. He was very tall and as he brushed the wisps of hair across his forehead with his fingertips, I could see his entrancing blue eyes. I flushed as a tingly sensation came over me. I felt almost giddy at the sight of him.

What is wrong with you? Pull it together.

"Ms. Jensen. I wanted to come by to apologize for my behavior this morning," he offered, coming a few feet closer, looking up at me, and gently running his hand over the rail of the porch.

"Oh well, in that case, please join me. And just so you know, this apology better be a good one," I said, turning quickly, hoping that the burning sensation I felt in my face wouldn't show. I grabbed the arm of one of the three rocking chairs that adorned the porch, sitting. I hoped this reaction would pass before he came any closer. *Geraniums*, red geraniums, that was what I would buy to put on the porch. I had no idea why that thought flew into my mind at this moment. Distracting myself, yes, that's what I was doing. I needed to think about anything else besides the man whose heat I could feel as he approached me.

Derek came up the porch steps and sat in the rocking chair beside me. *We could grow old together on this porch, sitting right here in these rocking chairs*. Wait. What? Where on earth had that idea come from?

"I wanted to talk to you about this house. You see my grandfather bought it in nineteen forty-six, six months after his wife, my grandmother, died. He was a single father to my dad and uncle, and they had lived in a much smaller house a few streets over. It was just six months later that he was killed in a car accident and my father and my uncle went to live with family in another town. They never even got a chance to move in." Derek explained softly.

"So, then my aunt Celia purchased the house from his estate?" I asked, confused, but at least I was starting to regain my composure.

"No, that's just the thing. The house was never sold," he explained.

"Well, then how did she come to live here?"

"I think she just moved in," he answered, starting to sound more like the man I met earlier at the diner.

That didn't sit right with me. In 1946, Celia would have been seventeen years old. Her family was not from Friendsville. They lived nowhere near here. No one in my family ever spoke about Aunt Celia being the black sheep and running away from home just to squat in some abandoned house. "And you're saying this because you have proof of that?" I challenged, my senses fully returned.

"Well...I mean, what other explanation could there be?" he stammered.

"There are plenty of reasons why she could have legitimately lived here. Do you have the deed to the house proving it was never sold?" I asked, wanting to suddenly defend Celia's honor.

"I haven't found it yet, but it's just a matter of time," he stated, indignance returning in his tone.

"Mr. Sullivan, Randy," I corrected, "said that the house is mine. Celia left it to me in her will. So, unless you have some proof that this house that she lived in for the last seventy-plus years was not her house, I suggest you get off my property."

I felt my anger rising. I felt my face flushing for a completely different reason this time. I have never liked confrontation, so I had no idea where this was coming from, but I was not about to back down. *Do not mess with an angry redhead.*

Derek started to speak, but it came out as a croak. He had no comeback because he had no proof. Instead, he abruptly rose to his feet and left the porch returning to his truck without another word.

I felt incredibly proud of myself. Did he think that I was just going to fall for his sob story about the house and just believe that Celia was some kind of a vagrant who stole it from his grandfather? I decided right then and there that I was definitely staying. This was going to be my house and I was turning it into a bed and breakfast after all.

Note to self: Google how to start a bed and breakfast.

Chapter Four

The next day I woke disoriented. I chose one of the spare bedrooms on the second floor of the house to be my bedroom for the time being. Randy mentioned that a housekeeper had been to the house to clean and change the linens, so the house was clean and the bedding fresh – not like a hotel where you try not to imagine the things that the sheets, or the bed for that matter, had been through. Clean though it was, the house just wasn't friendly. It was dank and stale and in dire need of some TLC. I decided that I was going to start my renovations or at least my brightening up of the place with the bedroom I was sleeping in. The money Celia left me would be plenty to do some modifications to the house.

First, I was going to need some breakfast and some groceries. The night before I took all my belongings out of the car and brought them into the house. I hadn't had the energy to actually unpack anything, so I took fresh clothes out of my suitcase and placed them on the bed. Did this place have a shower? A clawfoot tub maybe? I stepped out of the bedroom and found the bathroom down the hall. Thank goodness there was a shower and hot water. I would have to figure out how to put the utilities in my name so I would be sure to keep that hot water, not to mention the lights on. I added that to my ever growing to-do list.

Feeling renewed after showering and changing into fresh clothes, I decided to stop at Dotty's for breakfast and then to the market for groceries. My arrival at Dotty's was a completely different experience from yesterday's. Today Dotty greeted me by name with her signature coffee pot in hand.

"Good morning. Should I wait to be seated or seat myself?" I asked not wanting to wreck the good vibes I was getting today by committing a faux pas and having the whole town think I was an entitled city girl.

"Oh, darling we aren't formal here. Sit wherever you like," she said with a smile.

I smiled back and found an empty booth with a window view of the parking lot. Dotty was not kidding about this being an informal place. She followed me to the booth and sat in the bench in front of me. From my days as a waitress, I knew that sitting down at the table with the customers was not the professional thing to do. I turned my cup over thinking she was going to fill it or maybe she needed a break from standing. She did serve my coffee, but a break was not what she was after.

"Holly," she started, "I think you should know that Derek isn't normally like he was yesterday."

Oh no, where was this going? I hadn't considered the town's opinion of me moving into the house. No one seemed to be fond of Celia so why should I think that anyone would be on my side against Derek? This was not going to be good.

"So, he doesn't typically yell at strangers in public and show up at their house to yell at them some more?" I questioned.

"Oh dear no. That is completely out of character for him. He's a good boy but he has a lot on him lately. He has done more for this town than anyone has in the last thirty years. His intentions are good. In case you hadn't noticed, he is quite handsome too. If I were twenty years younger…." she trailed off with a quiet whistle. "He's single you know. I'm not sure why. Maybe he's tired of these small-town girls. Maybe he's looking for someone more worldly. Maybe someone just like you."

I had chosen that moment to take a sip of my coffee and nearly spat it out. Oh God, this was worse than I thought. Dotty fancied herself a matchmaker. I nearly laughed.

"Dotty, I appreciate you looking out for me, but I don't think I am what he is looking for. Actually, I am pretty sure he hates me," I answered truthfully.

"You know what they say about there being a fine line between love and hate, don't ya?" she sang, getting up from my booth and moving onto the next customer in need of coffee or maybe advice.

When Dotty came back to my table, I thought she would take my order, but instead she put a plate full of strawberry pancakes with a side of bacon on my table. "On the house," she said and walked away.

This is not what I typically would have ordered – I try to eat healthy, but I ate every-last bite and it was heavenly. I could just skip lunch, I thought. I probably would be full through dinner after that anyway.

Still sitting in the booth, I pulled a piece of paper and a pen from my purse. I was going to need to write down my to-do list if I was going to stand a chance of remembering everything. Groceries were next on my list. As tempting as it was to come here to Dotty's for every meal, I enjoyed cooking. If I ate here every day, I would weigh 900 lbs. I got up from my seat and waved to Dotty on the way out. She smiled and winked at me. I had to stifle a giggle. She was going to need to work on those matchmaking skills. Derek and me as a couple? Imagine.

On the way to the market, I got sidetracked by a sign in the hardware store window advertising a thirty-five percent off paint sale. A fresh coat of paint always brightened a room. Of course, that house was going to need much more than just paint, but it was a start and something I could do myself without having to figure out how to hire a professional.

I opened the door to the hardware store and was greeted by another jingling bell. That clanging sound was more pleasant than the greeting I received from none other than Derek Sterling who was standing at the counter. When he saw me he laughed like he had just heard a great joke and didn't want to share. I glared at him.

"Thanks buddy," he said to the guy at the register as he finished his transaction. "Still on for that beer this week?" The guy nodded and Derek stepped around me before he paused at the door.

"I hope you aren't buying anything to fix that house up. You will just be wasting your money," he barked, quickly exiting the door. I guess he wanted to get the last word in this time.

Ignoring whatever had transpired between us, the man behind the counter greeted me. "You must be Holly. I'm Ned. Ned's hardware," he said waving his arm to acknowledge the whole store. "What can I do for you?"

Unshaken from Derek's comment I answered confidently, "I'm going to turn Celia Anderson's house into a bed and breakfast, and I am going to have to fix it up first." It felt amazing to say that out loud. The whole morning, I kept thinking about how I might renovate the house and turn it into a workable space for the purpose I intended. Some walls might have to come down or maybe go up. I thought the house would be able to endure that. I had a feeling it had good bones.

I was not sure what Ned would think of that idea, still worried about the town taking sides. "This town could use a bed and breakfast," he answered and came around from the counter to talk about my options.

He was of course familiar with Celia's house, but like everyone else in town, with the exception of Randy, had never seen the inside.

"Listen, I am starting to branch out from the hardware store into more hands-on construction jobs. How about if me and one of my contractor buddies stop by the house tomorrow to look around? We can at least see what we could do with it," Ned suggested. "From what I can tell, the grounds are in pretty good shape," he continued. "It's just really overgrown. I don't know how you feel about that fishpond, but if you want to fill it in, it will have to wait. We only have two bulldozers in town and Derek just rented both."

I waived that admission off as odd. "I would love for you guys to take a look at the house tomorrow. Actually, the fishpond is one of my favorite features of the house. I definitely want to keep it."

"I would have to agree. I have some landscaper friends in town that could probably restore the pond and maybe even maintain it if you are interested," Ned offered.

"Really? Yes, that would be great too. Thank you," I answered.

"Take a look around and see if there is anything you need to get started."

"Thanks Ned. I'm really glad we met." I paused a moment thinking about how genuine the sentiment actually was. "Helping me isn't going to mess up yout beer night with Derek is it?"

Ned rubbed his chin. "Listen, Derek is actually a great guy. He is one of my best friends, but that doesn't mean I always agree with him."

I smiled and nodded, not sure of the meaning of that statement or if

I wanted to persue it further. Instead, I walked around the store to see if there was anything I could use right now. Since the paint was on sale, I decided I should at least look.

By the time I was ready to go back home, I had three cans of paint, painting supplies and a full week's worth of groceries in my car. I pulled up to the house feeling so productive and optimistic about my future. I felt like I was walking on sunshine. Until I saw what was in my yard. That momentary feeling of joy was utterly ruined and replaced with… worry? No. Anxiety? No, that was not it either. Rage. Yes, that was the feeling – rage.

Sitting in the backyard of my soon-to-be bed and breakfast were two bulldozers pointed directly at my house. I walked over to them to see if anyone was around and by anyone, I meant Derek Sterling. I remembered Ned saying that Derek rented the only bulldozers in town. Silly me. I thought it must have been to use them for important town council business. I didn't find him, but I did find a note. The note read: You have three days to surrender this house or these bulldozers are going to knock it down anyway.

I was tempted to storm into the house, but just in case Derek was watching from somewhere to get my reaction, I was not going to give him the satisfaction. Instead, I quietly walked back to my car and made three calm trips into the house with the groceries and the paint. Then once inside I immediately called Randy to see if what Derek was threatening was even legal.

"Holly, it is absolutely not legal to bulldoze a house while someone is occupying it." Randy assured me. "I will keep an eye out for any injunctions or anything that Derek might try to do to force you out of the house. This is just an attempt to intimidate you." *Sure, you don't have two large excavating vehicles pointed at the house you are sleeping in.*

"Well it's working," I replied.

"It is your legal right to get a restraining order against Derek and I could potentially have him arrested for trespassing." he offered.

I thought for a minute about the satisfaction I might get from having Derek arrested for trespassing, but that would start a war. My gut told me that Randy was right, and Derek was just trying to alarm me. "No, that won't be necessary."

"Okay then. Call me if you need anything else," Randy said before hanging up the phone.

I needed to keep my mind off the bulldozers in my yard, probably destroying the grass, and not let Derek intimidate me. I put my groceries away. Then, trying to distract myself with a project, I got all my painting supplies out to start painting the staircase.

The staircase was beautiful – the focal point of the living room. In its current state, the spindles were a shade of dingy gray that you could tell was once a bright white. I was going on a mission to return them to their former glory.

I went into the bedroom and dug around in my suitcase to some work clothes – jeans, an old Green Day t-shirt and sneakers. I changed clothes and then began laying around plastic drop cloths on the stairs and the floor. I thought that I would have the floors and the stairs themselves redone, but I still didn't want to make a mess with the paint. Next, I arranged the rest of the supplies I had gotten from the hardware store and set myself up to paint.

I started at the top of the stairs with the spindles and painted the banister as I went along. It was cathartic to mindlessly paint. As I applied the pure white paint, the staircase immediately came alive again. I knew at that moment the house was going to be amazing when I was finished with it.

Feeling joy in my project, I happily hummed as I moved along the rail. I was two thirds of the way down the stairs when I stood up to paint that part of the banister. At that moment, the front door flew open with gusto. It was Derek with his usual entrance style just letting himself into my house. *Next time remember to lock the door.*

"Derek, who do you think you are? You can't just barge into my …" I began as I started toward him, ready to give him a piece of my mind, but as the words were coming out of my mouth, my foot slipped on the plastic drop cloths.

You know how an accident can happen so quickly that you don't really know what is going on, yet you feel things in slow motion at the same time? My thoughts were a jumbled mess as the seconds ticked by. Should I grab the banister? No, it's wet. It's better than dying in a broken heap at the foot of the stairs. What are the statistics of household accidents leading to death? One in a hundred? Is that number even right or did I make it up? Once, my thoughts cleared, I braced myself for the pain that was sure to come next.

But as I landed, I didn't feel pain. I was flat on my back only as far down the stairs as my body length. My head was on the step I had been standing on when I started falling, but not really on the step. It felt cushioned somehow. I opened my eyes to see Derek on top of me with his hands under my head and back like he had caught me just before I would have cracked my skull.

He hovered over me. His breath ragged on the side of my face. His heart racing in his chest directly on top of mine. His body rigid against me. I searched his face for answers. When I brought my eyes back to his, his body relaxed, but he kept his arms around me.

He drew his face closer to me and brushed his lips softly over mine so that I could barely feel the warmth of his skin. He pulled me tighter into his arms and I cupped his face between my hands.

He leaned into me again, but this time he kissed me with longing and hunger. With a passion of a lover just returned home from a long absence. I couldn't do anything but kiss him back with the same intensity. It felt familiar, yet new. It felt like I had waited so long for this. *Had I been waiting for this?* I was feeling emotions of joy and hope and… *love? What was going on?* A minute ago, we were enemies and now embracing like lost lovers? It didn't make any sense.

Breathlessly, Derek spoke, "I…I can't stop," he confessed then continued to devour my lips with his.

I couldn't stop kissing him either. I wrapped my arms around him and pulled him even closer. I couldn't get enough. I could feel him against me, yet I felt like I was out of my body watching from far away. I felt disconnected somehow. Like the emotions I was feeling were not mine. *Did I really hit my head, and this is all a dream?*

We continued for minutes or maybe it was hours. Time had ceased to exist. The edges of the world around us blurred again.

Then like a fog lifting, the desire, the hunger, the longing, the love was just gone.

Derek stopped and pulled his lips from mine like someone had turned off the magnet that was forcing them together. He looked down at me again and froze for a moment. It was like he was searching my eyes for an explanation of what happened or looking for an answer as to what to do next.

I groaned, physically remembering that I had just fallen down the stairs. I was assessing my body to find any pain that might signal that I had broken something. The only thing I felt was the weight of Derek's body. He must have realized at the same time he was still on top of me and bent his knees to kneel beside me. With the hand that was under my head he gently guided me into a sitting position. We stayed there like that for a few moments in silence.

Finally, Derek spoke first. "Are you hurt?" he asked softly with genuine concern.

I assessed again before answering. "No."

He twisted himself around to sit next to me on the same step. "You really shouldn't use plastic drop cloths on the stairs – too slippery and dangerous," he chided.

I nodded in agreement. Then he stood and headed to the door.

"Wait," I said, not wanting him to leave without talking about what just happened.

He fumbled with the door knob for a few seconds before finally getting the door to open. He turned toward me as he widened the gap, his was hair disheveled and his lips still pink from the kiss.

"I don't know what that was, and I don't care. It doesn't change anything. You still have three days." With that he walked out the door.

Chapter Five

*E*arly the next day Ned and his friend came to the house as promised. Measuring and taking pictures of every room, they told me they were going to work up some plans and come back later so that we could talk about what I wanted. The problem was that I was not exactly sure what I wanted. The disclosure of this fact seemed to inspire both of them. So far, I told them that I wanted to convert the house into a bed and breakfast and that I needed the bedrooms to be used for potential guests and I needed a dining area that could accommodate ten to twelve people at a time. I thought I might want to convert the detached garage in the back into a living space for me – like the caretaker's quarters so I wouldn't have to use a bedroom in the house that could be reserved for guests. By the time they left, I think we were excited by the project.

I asked Ned for one more favor before he left, and it was a big one.

"Ned, I guess you saw where Derek parked your bulldozers," I started.

Ned hung his head in either real or mock shame. I couldn't tell. "Yes, they were hard to miss as I pulled into the driveway. Derek told me that he was going to use them as bargaining chips with the lady who was trying to take over his grandfather's house. That was before I met you. I'm sorry. I should have told him no."

"You can make it up to me. Do you have a spare set of keys?" I asked with a diabolic smirk on my face.

"Um, yes," he said weakly. I convinced him to give me the keys so that I could move them elsewhere. He dropped them into the palm of my hand before I hopped into one.

"Have you ever driven a bulldozer before?"

"Nope," I confessed. How hard could it be?

Ned groaned and gave me a quick lesson. Right foot brake, left-hand joystick to steer, do not touch the right joystick, which lifts the blade, or anything else in the cab. I gave it a try. It was thrilling and scary, but I was moving it. When Ned saw that I was moving it toward the street he started yelling and waving his hands wildly to get me to stop.

"Holly, where are you going?" Ned asked, his voice cracking from trying to yell over the noise of the bulldozer. "You can't just drive it down the street."

Apparently, as Ned described as patiently as he could, driving any distance on the road would destroy the chains and something about needing to add rubber to them if you wanted to do that. It was too much to take in just to make a counterpoint with Derek.

"I will get my truck and get them off your lawn since I sort of had to deliver them here…Sorry." He winced.

"Then I think you might owe me a favor," I said, not mad at him.

I convinced Ned, against his better judgment to park one of the bulldozers in front of the Town Hall. He didn't think it was a good idea, but he did it anyway. This time I was the one who left the note. It read: "Councilman Sterling, it seems you misplaced your bulldozer. You're welcome."

Feeling vindicated I left the Town Hall and returned home. Ned took the other bulldozer back to wherever it was he kept them. He told me that his friend was probably working on my house design the whole time we were "fooling around" with the bulldozers and that he would see me later.

Once back at the house, I decided to call my mother. I figured I had some time to kill since I doubted the architect was able to redesign a whole house that fast. I hadn't spoken to her since I arrived and I didn't text her details like she asked, so she probably thought I was dead. That's not true, but if I waited too much longer, she probably would send my dad to come to find me.

"Hi Mom," I said sheepishly when she answered the phone.

"Holly, thank God," she started. "Now that I know you aren't dead, where are you and what happened with the inheritance?"

I was relieved that she wasn't angry so there would be a better chance that she would be receptive to my new idea. "I'm still in Friendsville. Aunt Celia left me her house, everything in it and two hundred thousand dollars."

She hesitated for a moment then said, "Wow Holly, that's a lot. What are you planning to do with it?"

"I am going to stay here and I'm turning the house into a bed and breakfast. I'm sorry I didn't call you sooner, but I was caught up in finding contractors in the town to do some renovations and I then I started painting some of it myself," I said confidently. It wasn't like I needed my mother's permission to do what I wanted, however, feeling like she was disappointed in me was hard to deal with.

"I always thought that town could use a bed and breakfast." she said, but followed up with, "Are you sure you know what you are getting yourself into?"

Doubt set back in, but I tried to hold my ground. "I know this seems like another one of my whims, but it isn't. I truly feel like I'm supposed to be here."

"Good for you, Holly," my dad's voice came out of the phone. My mother must have put me on speakerphone as I regaled my big plan.

I told them more about the renovation and how there was a little pushback from someone in the town, but I assured them it was nothing I couldn't handle. I questioned my mother again about Aunt Celia and anything else she could remember about her or her life in Friendsville. The only other thing she remembered besides what she already told me before I left was that Celia was the principal of the elementary school for a long time. That would at least explain how she had $200,000 in her estate. Not having many bills or anything else to spend your money on, you could easily save that much.

"Promise me that you will educate yourself on how to run a bed and breakfast. All the past jobs you've had will have given you some knowledge, but you need more than just that," my dad insisted.

"You're right," I agreed. *Of course, he was right.* What did I know about running a B&B? I was going to immediately immerse myself in every class, seminar and YouTube video I could find.

"Good," Mom said, "We'll talk to you soon."

I needed to find out more about Celia too. Maybe the house held some answers.

Chapter Six

The attic seemed like a good place to start looking for clues about Celia's life. If the rest of the house was anything to go by, Celia wasn't a pack rat. Anything she put in the attic was likely something she didn't want to part with. For all I knew it could be empty, but I had a good feeling that there were treasures up there. All I had to do was release the ladder that led up to the creepy attic. I stared up at the ceiling frame and the pull-chain for a beat, hoping it wasn't full of spider webs and rats up there. I put my cell phone in my pocket because of my recent bad luck with stairs.

I pulled the chain and the attic ladder unfolded down to the floor. The stairs were sturdier than I expected and the attic much bigger. It was large enough to be an additional bedroom. While there was a good amount of dust, the room wasn't as dirty as I anticipated – not a single spider or rat in sight.

There was a bed though, along with trunks and boxes, old lamps, and other random furniture that were all antiques and could possibly be repurposed once again downstairs. I felt like I had found hidden treasure.

A beautifully crafted chest in a corner of the room caught my eye. It was made of cherry wood and adorned with a brass handle and hinges. It was a chest that may have once lived at the foot of a bed – like a hope chest. I feared that it was locked and if that were the case, the key could be anywhere. I tried the handle and to my relief and joy it opened right up.

The inside of the chest was lined in material with a large red and pink rose pattern. The chest was full of old letters and journals. There was also a handmade quilt. A quick Google search told me that it was a patchwork quilt with a bear paw pattern, common for the 1940's. The fabric patterns were all different, but the main colors were black, white, green, purple, teal and coral in various florals and patterns. It sounds like it would be ugly and too busy, but it all worked together to make a harmonious pattern. I lifted it out and spread it on the bed so I could see the whole thing.

I turned back to the chest and discovered that tucked carefully under the space that the quilt took up was a wedding dress. I pulled my hand back from it like it was fire. Celia had never married – at least no one ever told me that she had. There was so much that I didn't know about my estranged aunt. There were so many things that I feared no one knew about her. I was sure the answers to all my questions about her would be in those journals. Would it be a violation of her privacy to read her journals? I was torn.

It only took a few minutes for me to rationalize why I needed to read the journals. I needed to know more about my great-aunt and figure out why she left this place to me. Besides, was there really any chance I wasn't going to read them? C'mon.

The journals dated back to 1936 when Celia was just thirteen-years-old. She was extremely organized and started a new journal each quarter of the year. It looked like she wrote in them faithfully and put the date on each page. Her handwriting was ornate, and it took reading a few pages to get used to it. While I was intrigued by what Celia was like as a young teen, I skipped to the 1946 journal when the house was purchased. I wanted to know what was going on in her life at that time to try to figure out how she came to live here. I opened the journal and randomly picked a page to start.

March 14, 1946

It has been two weeks since I visited Emma in Friendsville – two weeks since I met Graham. I have been patiently waiting for a letter from him, but there has been nothing. Maybe he is busy with his boys. I know that Emma is wonderful at her job as a nanny for them, but there is nothing like a father's love. Maybe he has forgotten all about me. Maybe that day meant more to me than it did to him. He is, after all, a few years older than me and already had a wife and is wildly more experienced. But the connection between us was so strong. Wasn't it? I have never talked through the whole night with a man before. Maybe that just shows how inexperienced I am. For now, I will just wait and hope.

I was intrigued. There was more to great aunt Celia than I realized. I only knew her as an old lady and had to shift my mind to picture her in her youth. Dating in the 1940's sounded different and yet basically the same as dating in the present. You go out with someone. You like them. You have a great time and hope that they did too and then you wait for them to contact you. Obviously, in the forties the woman would always be the one who waited for the man and these days it wouldn't be shocking if the woman reached out first, but in the end someone is still waiting to see if the feelings they have are returned. I was thinking about what scenario would be more tortuous, then - waiting for mail to be delivered and knowing that it would take days to hear from your betrothed or now - checking your phone every five minutes waiting for a text. I think it's a tie.

I thought back to the day I met Derek when he barged into the diner and demanded Randy's attention. I remember he said his grandfather's name. At the time, I didn't care because I hadn't yet realized that what he was talking about directly involved me. He said that his grandfather's name was Graham. I was sure of it.

I paged back in the journal two weeks hoping to find out more about how Celia met Derek's grandfather.

March 1, 1946

I am so excited. I am visiting my best friend Emma in a place called Friendsville. It is three hours away from home. I am going to take the train and she is meeting me at the station. I am so happy for her and yet jealous that she took a job as a nanny so far away.

The train ride was lovely and exciting. I had never been on a train before. The conductor was very friendly and took my hand as I stepped off the train. I searched the crowd for Emma, and I found her almost immediately. I was not sure it was her for a moment because she was pushing a baby in a stroller and held the hand of the toddler next to her. Of course, they were the children she cared for, but I had not expected that she would bring them with her. Even more unexpected was the very handsome man who was holding the toddler's other hand.

Emma hugged me as soon as I reached her and introduced me to the children. Paul was the three-year-old and his brother Thomas was the baby. The handsome man turned out to be their father, Graham who had very kindly given Emma a ride to the train station to pick me up.

I could barely take my eyes off Graham. He had dark blond hair, blue eyes and stood nearly a foot taller than Emma beside him. His smile was what captivated me. When he smiled at me everyone else in the crowded train station disappeared.

Graham drove us all back to his house. It was a small brick house with red shutters and a white picket fence outlining the yard. I helped Emma put the children in their rooms for a nap and then she showed me to her room which I would share with her while I was staying there. Graham must have placed my bag on the bed while we were tending to the children. He left for work by the time we were in the kitchen ready for lunch. Emma told me that he was the town's sheriff.

Emma and I had a lovely day catching up at lunch and then caring for the children when they woke. We cooked dinner together and I wondered if Graham would be home to eat with us. He was not. But Emma and the children and I ate together before we bathed the boys and tucked them into their beds. Later Emma and I sat on her bed giggling like we used to - talking about the boys, who had become men in her absence, in our neighborhood. Emma asked about John Winston and what he was doing now. I always knew she was fond of him. Secretly, I hoped that meant she had no interest in Graham. We talked until we both fell asleep on her bed.

I woke a few hours later and could not get back to sleep. I crept out of Emma's bedroom and went to the kitchen to get a glass of water. Instead of going back to her room I sat on the sofa in the living room. Soon after, I heard Graham come home from work. He got himself a glass of water and came into the living room, stopping short when he saw me.

I greeted him and patted the cushion next to me. He secured his gun in a closet and then joined me on the sofa. Being so close to him, I felt tingly and giddy. We started talking, first about nothing – the smoldering ember in the fireplace and then how our days had gone, but soon no subject seemed to be off limits. We talked for hours. I learned that he was twenty-five-years old and that he was born in this small town of Friendsville. His wife died in childbirth with their son Thomas. He thought Emma was sent from God to help his family though he worried about appearances with her living in his house as they were not married.

We were surprised when the sun came up. It felt like we had only been on that sofa for minutes and here it was a new day. I told him that I needed to get back to Emma's room, so she was not worried about where I had gone. Before I walked away, I turned back and kissed him quickly on the lips then hurried back to Emma.

March 2, 1946

In what little sleep I had gotten, I dreamed of Graham and the sweet kiss we shared. Emma woke before me and started breakfast for everyone. I dressed and helped her so that she could prepare the children for the day. It was Saturday, her day off, but she wanted to make sure the children were dressed and fed.

Emma and I were going to spend the day shopping and maybe even catching a movie. She told me that Friendsville was not the place for such things, and we would have to go a few towns over. Graham graciously offered to drive us and then pick us up afterward. I noticed Graham looking at me all through breakfast and blushing and averting his eyes whenever I caught him.

We had a wonderful day, Emma, and I. We spent the time window shopping for beautiful dresses that we could not afford and sharing an ice cream sundae at the ice cream shop. That is when I asked her if she was in love with Graham. She nearly spit her ice cream at me, telling me that she did not think of him in that way at all. I told her I thought he was dreamy.

Graham made good on his promise to fetch us a few hours later and drive us home. The boys were so well-behaved for the car ride and all day for Graham as well. We arrived back at the house just about dinner time. The time seemed to drag on from there. I hoped that Graham and I would be able to be alone again after Emma and the boys went to bed.

After dinner, my sweet Emma served hot chocolate on the porch as there was still a nip in the air. She brought herself a cup too and then said it was too chilly for the boys to be out there and scooped up her cup and the boys and took them inside, leaving Graham and I together on the porch. I thought I caught a wink from Emma as she skirted the children in the house.

The air was crisp, and Graham suggested that I join him on the swing to keep warm. I gladly accepted, moving from my seat to the swing, bringing a blanket to cover us. We sat silently drinking our hot cocoa when I felt Graham take my hand and hold it under the blanket. We sat like that until the sun went down and the cocoa was gone.

We moved into the house and noticed that everyone else had gone to bed. He started a fire in the fireplace, and I welcomed the heat. Graham joined me on the sofa and under the blanket I brought in from the porch. He took my hand again and we talked into the night once again. This time it was about me and my hopes and dreams for the future. I told him that I thought of being a teacher, but that I really dreamed of falling madly in love and having a family of my own.

He pulled the blanket up higher around us and took my cheek in his hand. At first his kiss was a gentle brush over my lips as he looked into my eyes hoping I might want more. I leaned in closer to him signaling that I did indeed want more. He pulled me onto his lap under the blanket and kissed me deeply, caressing my body as he did. We stayed there until the fire burned out.

March 3, 1946

I joined Emma, Graham, and the boys at church the next day. I felt like every eye in the parish was on me. Who was this extra girl with Graham Sterling? They probably thought. It is bad enough that he lives with one woman who cares for his children and now two? I laughed to myself thinking about what they would say if they only knew the truth of last night.

After the service, it was time for me to catch my train and return home. I was deeply saddened. I wanted to have more time to spend with my friend of course, but now I had another reason not to want to leave. I thought my heart would break if I had to leave Graham. Emma took the boys out of the car first to show them the trains, leaving me alone in the car with Graham. She was really the best friend. I tried to hold back my tears as Graham and I said our goodbyes. He kissed me so thoroughly in the front seat, it felt like he was trying to make the feeling last until we met again. We promised to write to each other as I got out of the car. I said goodbye to Emma, Paul and Thomas and got on the train for home.

March 15, 1946

A letter from Graham came today!

It was just as I had hoped. He felt the same way I did. In his letter he told me that he had not stopped thinking about me since I left – that he was so lonely without me. Apologizing for not writing sooner, he explained that he was trying the whole time to figure out how we could *be together. He told me that he used all his savings to buy a bigger house on Maple Street in Friendsville where he and I and the boys could all live together. He was waiting for all the paperwork and other things to be taken care of, but once the house was his he would call for me to join him and then we could be married. If, of course, I was willing. "Of course, I'm willing!" I yelled joyfully at the letter.*

I fear that you, diary, and maybe my dear friend Emma are the only ones I can share this news with. I certainly cannot tell Mother and Daddy because they would never approve. They would say I was being taken advantage of, that it was all happening too fast and probably that he was only looking for a mother for his children. I also cannot tell Alice, my sister, either for fear she would spill the secret. I know in my heart that this is right, and that Graham loves me as much as I love him.

I must go for now to write Graham and tell him that I cannot wait to be his wife! Mrs. Celia Sterling.

Celia's story was finally making sense. I couldn't stop reading. I needed to know everything. It was such a beautiful love story. I looked at my phone to see that I had been in the attic for hours. Ned and his contractors would be coming back to go over the changes to the house any time now.

I decided to read just one more passage before putting the journals down for the night. I picked up the journal from the summer of 1946 and skipped to July, thinking they probably were getting settled in the house by then. As I started reading, I discovered with racing realization, that the story in this passage sounded so familiar that it was eerie. I could barely read it fast enough. As I got to the end of that diary entry I just sat, chilled to the bone.

My phone rang and startled me. It was Ned apologizing that his team was not going to be able to come by today. There was a glitch in the software, and they lost everything and had to start over. He said they would try to come by tomorrow. Instead of feeling annoyed or disappointed, I felt relieved. There was something else I desperately needed to do.

I climbed down from the attic, googled his number and immediately called him.

"Hello," said Derek.

I almost hung up. Not only had we not spoken about what had happened the day before and I was feeling a little childish about the bulldozer prank I had pulled earlier, but what I was about to tell him was unbelievable.

"Derek," I started, "it's Holly."

"Oh," he said smugly, like he was expecting me to call. "A call already and it's only day two."

Clearly, he hadn't been by Town Hall yet. "Can you come over?" I asked impatiently.

"Um, why? I mean you can just leave and tell Randy to turn all of the paperwork over to me."

"No, that's not why I am calling," I answered, annoyed at his arrogance.

"Listen if you want to talk about what happened yesterday…" he started and trailed off.

"No, I don't. I mean I do, but not exactly," I stammered. I needed to talk to him in person. Then I had an idea that I thought might appeal to him. "I found a chest full of Celia's documents. I want you to come over and help me go through them. Maybe the deed is in there."

He paused for a moment before answering. "Okay, let me tie up some loose ends here and I will be over around five thirty, okay?"

"Perfect," I answered, "I'll see you then."

I was nervous about him coming over and yet I could hardly wait. It was not because I was hoping for another moment like the one on the stairs. I had found out some information and he was the only person in the world who could appreciate it. I wondered if I would have the courage to say it out loud.

Derek arrived at five thirty on the dot. I was surprised to see that he brought pizza, soda, and beer. That seemed like such an odd gesture from someone who was trying to run me out of town. Maybe he was really the good guy that Dotty and Ned described him to be and this bad guy act was too much for him to keep up. Once again, I was feeling guilty about the bulldozers. Maybe I should just confess. *That will have to wait. I had more important things to tell him.*

"I wasn't sure how long it would take to get through the papers, and I was starving. I thought you might be too," he explained about the dinner.

"Yes, I am. Thank you. So, what's the beer for?" I asked.

"I wasn't sure if this was going to be a civil collaboration or if we were going to have to be drunk to get through it," he smiled, a stunning smile. He was charming when he was not being an ass.

I laughed. "I will start with soda and let you know," I joked.

It was his turn to laugh. I started to lead him to the attic. As we got to the staircase he paused. Noticing, I stopped mid-way up. He was waiting for me to clear it before he would start walking up. "Seriously?" I asked.

He just shrugged. "You can never be too careful. Not sure we should risk a repeat of yesterday."

His voice was playful, and I wasn't sure how to respond so I continued up the stairs. When I got to the landing, he started up, so we weren't on the stairs at the same time, just in case.

"You are ridiculous," I told him, laughing. "Was the kiss really that bad?" I dared to ask.

He shrugged and answered with a teasing grin, "I've had better."

"What?" I asked, faking indignance. He put an elbow on top of the pizza box he was holding and tried to cover his smile with his hand.

Truthfully, I thought the kiss was amazing. I wondered if he thought so too. I could still almost feel his lips on mine. But it didn't matter because it wasn't going to happen again. I just needed to focus on how I could stay on his good side right now.

I pulled down the hatch to the attic. He handed me the pizza and drinks and pulled the rest of the stairs down to the floor. He climbed to the top and then leaned down to take the pizza and drinks from me so that I could climb up. He was a gentleman at least. I was starting to not hate him quite so much.

Once I got to the top, we put dinner on one of the many abandoned tables that was clear of clutter. Derek took a slice and a napkin and offered one to me as well. I couldn't eat. I needed to jump right into it.

"I sort of brought you here under false pretenses," I started. I saw him immediately look over my shoulder at the bed behind me and then back to me. "No, not for that," I said sharply.

He had a look on his face that I couldn't read. Relief or disappointment? I couldn't be sure.

I took a deep breath and began my story. "When I came up here today, I found Celia's hope chest," I said, pointing to the open chest that was pushed up against the wall next to the bed. "It isn't exactly full of paperwork like I said. It is full of her journals – her diaries."

"Okay," he interjected. "Am I to assume you read some of them?"

"Yes, I read a good bit of them. I couldn't stop reading. Here is the short of it. Celia met your grandfather when she was visiting her friend who was your dad and uncle's nanny after their mother died. Celia and your grandfather fell in love. He bought this house for them to move into after they were married," I blurted.

"What?" he asked, putting down his pizza and wiping his chin with his napkin. "Are you sure it was my grandfather? Are you sure it was this house?"

"Your grandfather's name was Graham, right? And your dad and uncle are Paul and Thomas?" I asked, fact checking.

"Yes, that was my grandfather's name and my dad is Thomas," he confirmed.

I could see the disbelief on his face, so I pulled out the first journal and showed him the important passages. After going through several of them, he sat back on the floor and pushed against the table, running a hand through his hair.

"They were in love?" he asked. "Why wouldn't my dad ever have mentioned it?"

"Maybe he didn't know. He was the younger brother, right? So, he was only an infant at the time. Celia didn't tell anyone in my family. Maybe no one else in your family knew their plan either or maybe they didn't agree with it. Celia and Graham met only six months after your grandmother died," I said, offering potential explanations.

I opened the trunk again and pulled out the wedding dress I found as additional proof. I let the shock of all of this sink in with him for a while before dropping the bomb that I felt ticking inside me. I calmly grabbed a slice of pizza and a soda and sat next to him on the floor. We talked through more of what we had just read and came up with other theories as to how Celia came to live in the house by herself for so many years.

"We are just going to have to read all of the journals to find out the truth. I feel kind of bad about it – like we are invading her privacy," he admitted.

"I've read a bit further than what I shared with you," I confessed standing up, grabbing a beer, and handing it to him. "Here, you might need this."

Chapter Seven

"Uh, okay," he said, reaching for the beer and taking my word for it.

"I got up to the part where Celia moved from her family home to this one and was starting to decorate. I will just read this part to you...

"July seventh, nineteen forty-six.

"I finally had all my things moved into the house. It was so exciting to be able to start decorating. Graham was going to have all his furniture moved to this house after we were married. He told me that if I didn't like it, we wouldn't have to keep it. I didn't care how the furniture looked. I was so happy that Graham and I were going to be together that it didn't matter.

"He didn't like the idea of me living in the house all alone, but it was not proper for us to live together until we were officially married. He agreed to let me stay here alone, but he stopped by every day to visit with me and make sure I was okay. I loved that about him.

"Today, I was painting the spindles on the staircase. I knew it was just about the time when Graham would be checking in, but when he opened the door it gave me a start. I lost my balance and began to fall. Graham must have dashed to the stairs just in time to catch me.

"He cushioned my head with his hand, so I didn't hit it on the step. I was shaken but not injured. The two of us were lying there on the stairs for a second before he scooped me up into his arms and kissed me. Graham is a wonderful man. I love his kisses. I love him. I felt like we could have stayed there forever in each other's arms. It was so passionate that we almost lost our way. But Graham who is always the gentleman stopped before we went too far."

I stopped reading and looked at Derek. I hoped he would see that what she described was exactly what happened to us on the stairs yesterday. By the look in his eye, he at least thought it sounded familiar.

"I know that you didn't want to talk about what happened on the stairs yesterday," I started, "but this explains so much."

"Does it?" he asked, looking perplexed. I gave him a moment to process. I could see the wheels in his head turning as he thought about it. "Wait, so what you are trying to say here is that you think we were possessed by the spirits of Celia and Graham?" he asked, only half laughing.

"Yes?" I said, my voice pinched. I partially covered my face with the journal knowing that I sounded insane. But maybe I should have listened more to my mother when she talked about her connection to the spirit world. "Do you have a better explanation because I'm guessing you didn't just take one look at me at the diner and fall madly in love with me? Or maybe you did, I am pretty cute." I placed the journal on my lap and gave him my best Instagram-worthy duck lips.

He smiled and rolled his eyes at me.

"But seriously, what do you think? You aren't going to hurt my feelings," I assured him.

He ran a hand through his thick hair before speaking. "Okay. No. I mean I don't think so, but you're talking about ghosts here. Do you know how ridiculous that sounds?" he asked.

"Yes, of course, I do, but I did feel out of my body. When you were kissing me, I felt emotions that didn't feel like my own. You even said that you couldn't stop. Was it because you were so into it or because something wasn't letting you stop?"

"Okay, hand me that journal," he requested. I did as he asked, and he skimmed through more of it, past the part I had read up to. "So, if your theory is right, if we act out something else that she writes about in her journal they should possess us again?"

"I don't know. I'm not claiming to be an expert on paranormal behavior or anything," I said with a laugh.

"Okay, then let's try it. Do you trust me?" he asked, reaching for my hand to help me off the floor. That was a loaded question.

"Ha. Maybe," I said, hesitantly taking his hand and getting to my feet.

"Great. Get on the bed," he instructed with a smirk as he fanned his arm out toward the bed in front of us.

I was not completely sold on my theory. I had no idea if we could just conjure the spirits of our dead relatives just by uttering a few familiar words. I also was not comfortable with the idea of being in a compromised position with the man, who just hours before was a complete jackass to me. No, I didn't trust him at all. I did trust Celia, however. She had strong feelings against Graham moving in with her before they were married. Her virtue must have been important to her. Whatever this scenario Derek found and wanted to act out was not going to be one that compromised Celia's principles. I was sure of it. Kissing Derek was not the worst thing in the world either. I mean for educational purposes only of course.

After my brief pause, I hopped up on the bed and sat with my legs dangling waiting for instruction. Derek was clearly amused and raised one eyebrow watching me boldly get on the bed. He read the passage over again silently to make sure he got the words right. Then he placed the journal face down on the table to hold the page.

"Ready?" he asked. I nodded. "Okay, so you need to lay down on the bed sort of on your left side."

I did as I was told and asked, "Like this?"

"Yeah I think so," he responded. It was not like her journals were written like a movie script with stage directions, so he was just guessing.

"Okay, so when you see me standing at the foot of the bed, you need to roll over to your back and look at me. Then you say, 'Graham, it's so late. I was worried you weren't coming over tonight.' Got it?"

I nodded. I wanted to ask what was supposed to happen, but I was afraid I would forget my line.

"Okay, then I will say my thing and we will see that absolutely nothing happens because this is ridiculous." He sounded so sure of himself.

I wanted to argue that I was not completely solid on this theory either. I wanted to tell him that I hoped he was right because the last thing I wanted was to have to kiss him again. Not exactly true, but he didn't need to know that. I wanted to tell him to just leave. Why did he even want to do this – just to prove me wrong? But I didn't. I rolled to my side and thought about the exact words I was supposed to say.

I felt him leave the side of the bed and walk to the other side of the room. I heard him take a deep breath and then his footsteps coming closer to the bed. When I heard him stop, I rolled over slightly to my back, looked at him as he stood at the foot of the bed, and said my line. "Graham, it's so late. I was worried you weren't coming over tonight."

He stepped closer to the bed, and said, "I couldn't stand to be away from you for even one day."

For a second it felt silly like we were rehearsing for cheesy community theater and the lines were too sappy to be what anyone would say in real life. Until a feeling came over me. It was like a dream state when you are just about to fall asleep, but you are still on the brink of consciousness and still aware of your surroundings. I felt peaceful and happy - no, not just happy, I felt joyful. Then it was like a magnetic force was pulling on us, Derek bent down to kiss me. I hungrily returned the kiss and pulled him into the bed. His eyes were wide at first with the surprise that this was happening and then he closed them and kissed me deeper. I felt an intense ache, needing to touch him. I pulled away from him for a moment and lifted his shirt over his head. He helped me remove it and tossed the shirt off the bed. I ran my hands over his muscular arms as he kissed my throat and moved down to the top of my chest. I felt a passion and desire like I had never experienced before. He paused and looked into my eyes like he was searching for permission to do whatever was going to happen next. I had no control. It was Celia's call and she was more than a willing participant. Immediately, he worked the buttons on my shirt until it lay open around me. He cupped my bra with his hand and kissed my lips again with hunger. I moaned at his touch.

At that moment, Derek's cell phone rang from the table across the room. Everything suddenly halted and we woke from our dream state. The spell was broken. It was like someone turned off a switch, but at the same time, our bodies were still reacting to each other. One tender releasing kiss and then we parted while trying to catch our breath.

The cell phone stopped ringing and then immediately began ringing again like someone was desperate to reach Derek.

"You should get that," I said, pulling my shirt around me to cover myself.

Derek stood and in one motion pulled his shirt back on and reached the other side of the room to pick up his phone. "Hello?" he muttered into the phone, sounding like the person on the other end had just awoken him. In a way they had.

"What? How did that happen?" he asked, raising his voice in what sounded like alarm. "It's okay. I'll be right there." He disconnected the phone and looked straight at me. His face was red with anger or was it flushed? It could have been either.

"Holly," he started, "I can't think about this right now. I have an emergency and I have to go."

"Is everything all right?" I asked, even though his use of the word emergency clearly stated everything was not, in fact, all right.

"It's just something I have to take care of now," he gathered his things and started to head toward the attic steps. He stopped and looked at me. "I'm sorry I can't stay to discuss this. But, I have to say I didn't believe it before, but now I do."

With that, he disappeared down the attic steps.

I sat on the bed for a few minutes after I heard the front door close. There were so many feelings going on inside me and not all of them were mine. It was troubling to try to sort them out. There was Celia's great love for Graham projected onto Derek. There was the Derek of the last two days who was trying to intimidate me. Then there was the Derek of tonight who brought pizza and shared in Celia's experiences. Then there was the scene that played out on the bed. Was it really Celia and Graham, or was it Derek and me, or a twisted version of both?

I remembered the journal that was sitting on the table and I had to read the entry to find out what might have happened if Derek's phone hadn't rung. I took it off the table and sat back on the bed. The diary read like a playbook for what just happened between us. I tried to remember if I removed Derek's shirt first as Celia had done to Graham. I think I had. Was that just a reaction or was Celia truly here through me? It was surreal.

I kept reading waiting to find out what had stopped them because my virtuous aunt never would have had sex before marriage. She had promised herself that much. I read more and while she was not graphic in her details, the final line in the entry told the whole story. *"I gave myself to him tonight because he is my soulmate and I know that we will be together forever."*

I threw the journal on the bed. I couldn't decide who I was angrier with – Celia for breaking her own promise or Derek for playing with fire. Celia was in love. I needed to give her some grace for that. Maybe Derek didn't read the last line to see how it ended. He said he didn't believe what I thought to be true so maybe he didn't think it would even matter.

Collecting myself and cleaning up the pizza and drinks, I climbed down from the attic, threw away the trash and put the leftovers in the refrigerator, then went to my bedroom. Sitting on the bed I laughed. Of course, I had inherited a haunted house. That was just my luck. Somehow, I wasn't afraid. I should have been creeped out and left, giving the house to Derek, but I wasn't. I felt like the house was part of me and I needed to protect it.

Chapter Eight

Ned and his friend Charlie arrived at my house at 9:06 a.m. the next day. I'm almost ashamed of how surprised and impressed I was with the technology they had. I felt like I was on HGTV and was having Chip and Joanna remodel my house.

Using the 3D model, we went room by room to discuss changes and updates. They had come up with some great ideas and I realized as I got into it that I had a vision of what I wanted after all. We decided the only thing we needed to do to the five bedrooms was update them with new paint and a few minor repairs that needed attention. Downstairs, they suggested opening the floor plan. They were going to remove the inside wall of the kitchen so that it would expand into the existing dining room, tripling its size and then remove the front wall but add a countertop bar that would split the kitchen from what would become the dining room. The living room would become more of a sitting area and the fireplace would remain while building in some bookshelves and a place for a TV in case guests wanted to have some activities to do at night other than being confined to their guest rooms.

"Charlie, what do you bet that there are original hardwood floors under these carpets?" Ned asked.

"Oh, one hundred percent they are," Charlie answered Ned, then turned to me. "In the forties, hardwood floors were out of style so everyone covered them up with carpet. Today, people would kill for hardwoods."

"Well, what are you waiting for?" I asked. "Rip up a piece."

Charlie looked at me like I just gave him a winning lottery ticket. "You sure?"

I nodded and Charlie took out his pocket knife to pull up a corner of the carpet. I could tell by the look on his face he liked what he saw.

Ned stepped closer to get a look and let out a slow whistle. "Holly, these floors are definitely hardwood and in solid condition. We could buff these up and stain them and they would be as good as new."

Happy with the win, I pursued an additional idea. "So, what do you guys think about converting that detached garage in the back into my living quarters?"

"That's not a bad idea. It would take a total rebuild to make that space livable, but it is doable. Don't you think Charlie?" Ned answered.

"I don't see why not. The improvements we are talking about making to the house won't use up your whole budget," Charlie started, "but the thing about these old houses is that sometimes unforeseen issues come up and then suddenly you are over budget."

Ned nodded in agreement. "Maybe we should finish the rest of the house first. We can price it out for you, but then keep that line item open in the budget just in case. Then we can address it later."

I needed to mentally prepare myself for something like that to happen. I mean it happened in just about every episode of every home improvement show. I hoped that was just to add drama to the shows, but I kept the possibility in the back of my mind anyway. I was feeling confident that since everyone kept telling me how much this town needed a bed and breakfast, I would make back my investment someday.

"I think that is a smart idea to hold off," I agreed. "I am so excited about this project! Thank you so much for all your help."

As I walked them out, Ned pulled me aside. "I got an early call this morning from the mayor asking me to remove the bulldozer from the Town Hall," Ned said matter-of-factly.

"Oh no. I didn't get you in trouble, did I?" I asked, worried that everyone in town was going to be mad at me.

"Nah, I installed a pool at the mayor's house below cost last year. He kind of owes me," he said. I felt a rush of relief. "To be honest, I think he thought the whole thing was funny, but he just couldn't have it sitting out there for the whole town to wonder about it. He said he wasn't sure if Derek saw the sign, but he put it on his desk."

"I'm glad to hear the mayor has a sense of humor. Do you really think Derek was going to knock down my house?" I asked, feeling like that was unlikely, but thought I would check anyway.

"Well, I hear he has a plan for reinventing the town to attract more tourists. The rumor is he has deals in the works with major business owners that are going to build around here and this house is smack dab in the way of all that. Before you came here to claim the house, he was going to have it knocked down and the land made into a parking lot," Ned explained and then got into his truck.

I was feeling two things – rage and hunger. I decided to go to Dotty's instead of cooking breakfast for myself like I had planned and hoped I didn't see Derek, or I may have punched him. On second thought, maybe I decided to go to Dotty's hoping I did see him. I was ready for a fight.

Walking to the diner seemed like just the thing to calm me down. It wasn't far from my house, and I hoped walking in the fresh air would help clear my head. There was a church a few blocks down from my house on the way to the diner. It was a beautiful white church with a tall steeple and red doors. The parking lot was empty. It wasn't Sunday and daily mass had been over for an hour according to the sign in the front lawn. I stopped to look at the trees that surrounded it. The ground was wet from a soaking rain we had in the middle of the night. I walked slowly, deeply inhaling the clean air that always followed a rainstorm.

As I passed the trees, I saw something out of the corner of my eye. As I got closer, I realized it was someone huddled under the partially covered staircase of the church that lead to the front doors. It was a boy about ten-years-old clutching his knees and shivering. I hurried over to him to see if he was hurt or lost. I approached gently so I wouldn't scare him away.

"Hello," I said to him softly. "Are you okay?"

He raised his head to look at me. He was soaked. He must have been there through the night weathering the storm. His face was wet, but I wasn't sure if it was raindrops or tears. I feared it was the latter.

"Hey, I'm Holly," I said reaching a hand out to him. "What's your name?"

He took my hand and crawled out from his hiding spot. "I'm Sam," he told me.

"Sam, are you lost? Have you been here all night?"

He just looked away trying not to let me see him cry. I spotted an overflowing donation box in the parking lot. I walked over to see if I could find him some dry clothes. I found some jeans, a T-shirt, and a hoodie. I told him to come over and change into those clothes behind the donation box. He was so cold that he did as I asked.

"Sam, are you hungry?" I asked, knowing that he had to be starving. "I'm going over to the diner for some breakfast. Would you like to come with me? My treat."

"No, I can't. They know me there. If they see me, they're going to call my uncle," he explained.

Now we were getting somewhere. I wanted to ask who his uncle was, but I hadn't met that many people in town to know them all by name anyway.

"How about if anyone asks, we tell them that your uncle knows we are having breakfast together and is going to meet us there?" I offered. I wasn't sure if lying was really a great idea, but I didn't want this boy to run away again either.

"Okay," he said, and we walked slowly to the diner without speaking. I wasn't sure what I was going to do next. I hoped that the neighbors at the diner would give me some clues. Did he run away a lot? Was his uncle abusing him? He looked well taken care of besides being weathered by the storm. In a town where everyone knew everyone else's business they surely would know something.

As I opened the door to the diner, I felt as though Sam was going to run, but instead he walked in first as I held open the door. Dotty, as usual, was in the front holding her coffee pot. If anyone knew this kid, Dotty would.

"Sam," she said right on cue, "how ya doing kiddo? Where's your uncle this morning?" Before Sam could say anything, Dotty saw me and beamed with delight. "Oh, you're with Holly. I see you two have met. Take a seat wherever you like."

So that was odd. Dotty thought nothing of Sam and I having breakfast together. Not to mention the fact he was wearing jeans that were two sizes too big and a hoodie big enough for an extra-large full-grown man.

We took a seat in a booth in the back. I made sure that I was on the side facing the door so I could see if anyone coming in looked panicked like they lost a child.

"What would you like to order?" I asked Sam, even though I was dying to get to the bottom of this. I knew that taking it slow and gaining his trust was what I had to do, or he would just take off again.

Sam decided on strawberry pancakes and chocolate milk. When I asked for the same, Sam's eyes lit up. I did ask for coffee though. I had a feeling this was going to be a long morning.

When I discovered him under the church stairs, I noticed that he had a black backpack with him likely holding all his possessions inside. What does the world of a ten-year-old boy look like? I wondered. I hadn't mingled much with pre-teen boys in my days of childcare. My experience in that realm was with preschoolers who thought the world was just like Daniel Tiger's Neighborhood – perfect. This boy had seen some things in his young life that maybe I hadn't yet in my thirty years. I could tell.

He scarfed down his pancakes like they were the best things he had ever eaten or like he hadn't eaten since lunch the day before. After devouring the pancakes, he wiped his mouth with his napkin and pulled a comic book out of his backpack. I had a glimpse into the world contained in his sack and something to talk about with him.

"You like comic books?" I asked stating the obvious. Wow I was bad at small talk with children.

"I just started reading them," he revealed, holding up a Marvel Ironman comic. "I really just like the movies, but my uncle thought I might like these too. They're okay I guess."

Superhero movies. Yes! I got this. I loved everything Marvel that came out in the movies and TV since 2008. I watched everything at least twice and it had nothing to do with Chris Hemsworth as Thor. Okay, maybe it did a little bit. I was a true fan of the whole francize.

I opened with, "I think Captain America was my favorite movie, although the Avengers with all of them working together is epic."

Sam's eyes widened with surprise and then he smiled at huge smile recognizing a fellow fan. "Yeah Captain America is okay, but Ironman is my favorite. He is so smart and confident. He's always like 'Do your worst you can't stop me.'"

"Yeah, but I really liked when Pepper had powers," I added. Sam got a confused look on his face. It was then I realized that the movies started coming out before he was born and while I caught them in real time he was probably just catching up.

"Oh," I backpedaled a bit. "So what movie are you up to?"

"Just the first Avengers movie. My dad and I started watching them together until…" he trailed off stuffing his comic book back in his pack. He seemed to be holding back tears and I wondered how he came to be here with his uncle. I feared it was not just summer vacation while his parents were on a trip. He looked like he was getting ready to take off again. I couldn't let that happen before getting him back to his uncle.

"Well I own all of the movies," I said. That was a half-truth. I had Netflix and Amazon Prime where I was sure I could access any of them. "Maybe we could watch them together some time."

His eyes brightened, "Okay, that would be great!" he said excitedly.

"Of course, we would have to get your uncle's permission," I stated, transitioning to the real matter at hand.

"Ugh," he said. "He probably won't let me. He just works all the time and leaves me with these lame old lady babysitters who act like robots. I hate him."

"Sam, I'm afraid you're going to have to tell me who your uncle is. He is probably worried sick about you. I need to let him know you're okay," I explained, hoping that he would give the information and not run. "I think I could probably just ask Dotty, but I would rather you tell me."

Sam sighed. "Derek Sterling. Go ahead and call him. You probably think he's the greatest guy just like the rest of the town," he answered, sounding defeated.

"Bleck," was the sound of disgust that escaped from my mouth. It was unintentional, but Sam seemed delighted. I continued. "I can't stand that guy."

"Why?" Sam asked, fascinated.

"Well, because he is trying to get me to give up my house so that he can continue with his plan to restore the town. I guess my house is in the way," I answered, trying not to make Derek sound like the worst guy ever. I didn't want Sam to feel that way about his uncle and honestly, I didn't really feel that way about him either.

A flicker of recognition sparked in Sam's eye. "You're the old lady who lives in the house on Maple Street? I've heard my uncle talk about that house and how it is really our family's."

"No, the old lady was my aunt who just passed away and left the house to me," I explained.

"He said it was an old lady who got the house from her aunt. I think he called you old," Sam announced and laughed feeling proud of himself.

I knew he was joking, but I played along. "Ugh, now I don't like him even more!"

Sam laughed. I knew it was time to call Derek. Maybe Sam running away was why Derek left so abruptly last night. If that was the case, I was going to have to forgive him for it. I pulled out my phone while still sitting in the booth with Sam and called Derek. I told him that I found Sam and that we were at Dotty's having breakfast. I could hear the relief in his voice as he told me he would be right over.

I ordered more coffee for myself and chocolate milk for Sam.

"Want to know a secret? Well, kind of a secret," I offered trying to kill time until Derek arrived.

"Sure!" Sam answered excitedly as I hoped he would.

"Your uncle and I are in a prank war," I started. *That was the better way of saying your uncle was trying to strong-arm me and I showed him.* "He started it by parking two bulldozers in my front yard. You know like trying to send me the message that he wanted to knock down my house." I left out the part about the warning note.

"No way!" he said. "So, then what did you do?"

I smiled and paused a beat for effect. "I tried to drive one of the bulldozers off the lawn, but you can't really drive them anywhere. So, I asked Ned from the hardware store to take one on his truck and park it in front of Town Hall and then I left a note," I explained.

"What did the note say?" Sam asked, wide-eyed.

I had to think about it to remember. "It said, 'Councilman Sterling, you seem to have misplaced your bulldozer.'"

"Oh my gosh. That is the best prank ever!" Sam said with glee.

"The only bad part was that the mayor saw it this morning and asked Ned to take it off the property. I'm not sure if Derek saw it, but Ned told me that the mayor put the sign on Derek's desk," I said, finishing the story of the escapade.

"Wow, you're like an Avenger," Sam cheered.

Suddenly, in Sam's eyes, I was a hero. Somehow moving to this small town gave me the courage to be the person I was always meant to be, and I liked the feeling. I couldn't believe a ten-year-old could make me feel happier, lighter, *braver*. We continued to talk more about our favorite superhero and waited for Derek to arrive. I was anxious and I think Sam was too. I had no idea how Derek would react.

About ten minutes later I saw Derek walk into the diner – well, I heard him first with his aggressive way of entering a room. He looked like he hadn't slept all night. He was still wearing the same clothes he had on when he left my house. His hair was flat and still damp like he had been out in the rain all night looking for Sam. For a moment I worried that he was the *bad uncle* that Sam had described but, seeing him now – with the tears in his eyes when he saw the back of Sam's head – I knew that he was just a guy who was trying to parent a kid, who wasn't his, the best way he could.

"Sam," Derek sighed as he reached our table. Sam hung his head and refused to look Derek in the eye. Derek pushed himself into Sam's side of the booth and hugged Sam like he never wanted to let him go.

I felt like it was not my place to be in this moment, so I got up without either of them really noticing and walked to the front to join Dotty where she greeted her customers.

"Such a tragedy," Dotty said, shaking her head as I approached her.

"What is?" I asked, wondering what part of the town gossip I had missed now.

"Sam's parents died in a car accident about six months ago. It was Derek's younger brother and his wife. Being Sam's godfather was something that Derek took very seriously and chose to take in the boy. A single guy raising a child with no experience is not easy. Derek is struggling, but he won't give up," she confided in me.

I may have audibly gasped. Even though I had the feeling that Sam was not just visiting, it was still a little shocking to hear the truth out loud. I saw Derek wave me back over to the table. I excused myself from Dotty and went back to my seat.

"Thank you, Holly, for finding Sam and keeping him safe," Derek said sincerely.

"It was nothing," I said. The cliché was the only thing I could think of to say.

Derek looked over at Sam. "If Sam would stop running away from babysitters we wouldn't be here right now," he said, messing with Sam's hair.

"I don't need a babysitter and even if I did you've picked the worst ones," Sam replied with an eye roll for extra effect.

Derek looked at me apologetically like he didn't mean to drag me into this drama. "Well, I work a lot and you can't be left by yourself all the time buddy. I am trying to do my best. Although, I think you may have run through all the possible nannies in town now anyway. I'm not sure what to do now."

"He can hang out with me," I heard myself say without really thinking about it. They both looked up from the table at me with the exact same expression which I took as surprise.

"Holly, I can't ask you to do that," Derek said.

Sam followed up with, "I told you I don't need a babysitter." He said it in a way that made me feel like I had betrayed him in some way.

"I didn't say I wanted to babysit you. I said that you could come over and hang out with me during the day. I am fixing up my house and I could use some help. It's not like it would be a free ride or anything. You would have to work," I said, laying it out on the table.

"And you," I started, referring to Derek, "can take your big three-day threat and shove it up your…" I looked at Sam and stopped myself from finishing that sentence. "I mean since neither of us have the deed to the house I propose that we call a truce until we find it. Also, you will have to come over for dinner every night and then after dinner we will all catch up on all the Marvel movies and TV shows."

What was I doing? I had no more experience parenting or supervising a ten-year-old kid than Derek did. But they were broken, and I wanted to help. I thought getting Derek to take an interest in what Sam was interested in was a good first step. I figured that Sam might want to help me with the house to anger Derek – *I remember that much from being a preteen myself.* Also, I could use the help and Sam might learn something from Ned and the contractors. A truce between Derek and I might help me figure out if he really is the great guy the townspeople say he is or the lunatic he was when we first met. It was a win all around.

"Uncle Derek, can I?" Sam asked excitedly.

Derek gave me an, "are you serious?" look to which I nodded yes. "Well, I guess if you want to waste your time helping with a house that's going to eventually get demolished that's up to you," he answered.

"So that is a yes?" I asked. "Including the truce with no more talk of demolishing the house?"

"Yes," Derek replied. Sam gave him a high-five.

"Oh, and by the way," Derek said, talking to me, "Great retaliation with the bulldozer. I saw it last night when I was combing the streets for this one." He pointed at Sam.

This time it was Sam and I who high-fived each other.

Chapter Nine

Sam started coming to the house every day. Derek would drop him off at 8 a.m. and Sam and I would get straight to work. The house needed so much care. It appeared Celia had changed nothing about the house since she finished decorating it seventy years ago. She also hadn't maintained it very well in the later years of her life. We didn't focus too much on the downstairs where most of the building renovation was going to happen but rather concentrated on the bedrooms that just needed cosmetics.

Sam was a dutiful helper. He never complained or said he was bored and wanted to play video games. He just did whatever I asked. We started with the bedroom farthest away from the stairs. It was also the farthest away from Celia's bedroom which was an issue I was going to have to deal with sooner or later.

Since I arrived, I still hadn't spent much time in that room. I peeked in every once and a while but never dared to go all the way in and always locked it when I left. It was the only room in the house that truly looked lived in before I got there. Her bed was made, but the sheets looked worn and instead of a fancy duvet there was a tattered pink blanket on top. There was still a clean teacup on her nightstand like it was awaiting her return. The top of her dresser was covered in neatly arranged items, including a hairbrush, perfumes, and other knick-knacks that undoubtedly had special meaning to her and a smattering of prescription bottles and arthritis cream.

The memory of the time Celia described in her letter of me visiting her as a child started to come back to me the longer I stayed in the house. She talked about how my grandmother and mother busied themselves in the kitchen while she sat in a chair in the living room – the one I climbed up onto to snuggle in her lap. I remembered that chair. It was winged back with big, bright pink and red florals that covered the entire chair. I thought it might have been upholstered in the same material that lined the chest in the attic. I noticed the chair was no longer in the living room and I thought perhaps in the last twenty-five years it had been discarded. Until I peeked a little farther into her bedroom.

Around the corner from the door was a small sitting area with a TV on an antique table and in front of that TV was the chair – her chair. The upholstery was no longer bright, but dingy like the rest of the house. The cushion looked worn and may have had a blanket or a pad on the seat. The night I discovered the chair was the last night I even peeked into the room. At some point, I realized that I was going to have to do something with that room. It couldn't just be the locked bedroom in the bed and breakfast that everyone just ignored. That didn't mean I couldn't save it for last though.

Sam and I were still working on the first bedroom. There was more to do in it than I thought. Celia never threw away anything. It took four whole days just to go through all the things. It didn't help that we kept stopping to look at all the treasures she had.

"Holly, look at this!" Sam would say every time we unearthed something historic. He didn't care much about the clothes – they were all out-of-date women's clothes to him. I was more fascinated by them. Celia must have been very stylish back in her heyday. She was also somewhat of a clothes horse. I wasn't sure what to do with all of them. This small town was not much for vintage clothing, but I knew there was a market for them somewhere. Thanks to Google, I found a vintage clothing shop about an hour away that was willing to take them on consignment. The store owner was beyond excited. Apparently, 1940s and 1950s apparel were making a comeback. I promised I would deliver the clothes as soon as we had found all of them. I had a feeling we just scratched the surface with this bedroom. So, for now, Sam and I were just gathering the clothes in bags and dragging them into the hallway.

"Hey Holly, look at this!" Sam shouted from deeper inside the closet. I couldn't wait to see what today's "look at this" find was going to be.

He was working on clearing out the floor of the closet now that the clothes weren't hanging in the way. He crawled out holding a box of yellowing newspapers. We sat on the bed and looked through them together. The newspapers had headlines like, "Man Walks on the Moon," "Berlin Wall Tumbles," "Nixon Resigns," and even "King of Pop is dead at 50."

There was one paper at the bottom that was a clipping instead of a full newspaper. This headline read "Local sheriff dies on icy road." I held it in my hand and stared at it. The article contained a photo with the caption "Graham Sterling was only two years into his term as sheriff." I stared at that photo. It was the first time I saw a picture of Graham.

He was handsome and had the same gleaming smile as Derek. As I read the details of Graham's accident in the article, I felt such anguish and despair that it took my breath away. *No, no. This can't be true.* The words rang in my ears. A sob was stuck in my throat and I wasn't sure if I could hold back the tears that were welling inside me.

"Holly, are you ok?" Sam asked, touching my shoulder. It took a moment to regain my composure. I must have been experiencing what Celia felt when she read the article. I felt her incredible loss. In one single moment, she lost her whole world – her future. It was beyond heartbreaking.

I let out a deep breath and answered Sam. "Sorry, yes I'm fine. I was just thinking how sad this is."

I realized that Sam was looking at the newspaper over my shoulder. "Was he related to me?" Sam asked, noticing they shared the same last name.

"Yes," I answered. "He would have been your great-grandfather."

"Oh," he responded, coming to his feet hanging his head. He was probably thinking about his parents and how they had similarly perished in a car accident.

"Sam," I said, softly touching his arm. "If you don't want to talk about it that's okay. Dotty told me what happened to your parents. I'm so sorry. I can't imagine what that must be like for you. Do you want to tell me about them? It's okay if you don't."

Sam raised his head and tears ran down his face. "I miss them so much," he managed to utter in between sobs.

I scooped him up in a giant hug and let him cry on my shoulder. He seemed like he was so busy fighting against Derek that I wondered if he had even mourned his parents yet. The emotion I felt from Celia moments before, helped me relate to Sam's sorrow. We stayed in the position for probably five minutes and I would have hugged him all day if it made him feel better. He pulled away though, wiped away his tears, and stood tall like a superhero. But he wasn't a superhero and he didn't need to be. He was a kid and should have been able to act like one.

"My mom and dad were great parents. They always took me everywhere with them. Except for that day I was in school and they were going to a convention for realtors. That's what they did – they owned a real estate company. They never made it to the convention. They were hit by an eighteen-wheeler truck," he said like he was reading from a script. He looked down again and started kicking at the floor with the toe of his shoe.

My skills were vast, but being a therapist was not in my wheelhouse. I hoped that Derek was taking him to counseling or at least some kind of grief support group.

"That's really awful," I said, "and really unfair. If you ever need to talk about it or talk about anything at all you can come to me. I'm not sure if I can always help, but I will always listen."

He sat down beside me on the bed again and put his head on my shoulder. I placed my head on top of his. It took a lot of my strength not to cry – for Sam and Celia. I appreciated at that moment what Derek was undertaking. Raising his brother's son as his own without hesitation. It wasn't easy to know if you were doing or saying the right thing especially with a kid who just lost his whole world.

After sitting there like that for a few minutes I felt like we needed to lighten the tension. "So, you are kind like Batman," I stated, referring to the only superhero I could think of who had lost his parents. "And that would make Derek, Alfred. So, he's like your butler."

Sam raised his head and snickered at the thought. "Holly, Batman is DC, not Marvel. I only know what you're talking about because everybody knows who Batman is."

"Sorry," I said, pushing the air with my hands, "I didn't realize you were a comic snob." He just shook his head at me with a smile he tried to contain.

"I think we've worked hard enough today," I declared. "Part of the deal with Derek is that we have to eat dinner together. We haven't started doing that. I think we should tonight. It's really funny that he never bothered to ask if I knew how to cook."

Sam gave me a look of fake, maybe a little bit real, concern. "Do you know how to cook?" he asked cautiously.

"I don't know. Let's find out," I teased.

Chapter Ten

*D*erek came to the house at 5:30 pm sharp as he did for the last couple of evenings to pick up Sam. There had already become a familiarity with the routine. Derek would just let himself in and walk through the house to find out where we were. Usually, Sam and I were either upstairs in one of the rooms still cleaning up and wondering where the day had gone or completely exhausted and resting on the living room furniture sitting on top of the bedsheets that the housekeeper tossed over everything and I hadn't bothered to remove.

Today, Sam and I were in the kitchen. It was a small galley kitchen which after the renovation would be my dream kitchen. For now, two people in the kitchen were pushing it. The stove and sink were together on one wall while the refrigerator and pantry were on the other, both sides lined with cabinets. There was no dishwasher and that was going to be one of the first things that changed.

Derek came walking in the door and paused at the entrance to the kitchen. I noticed him taking in the sight of me and my little sous chef working on dinner and laughing while we did.

"Well hello," Derek said with a smile. "Something smells amazing in here."

I prayed that Sam would still be smiling now that Derek had entered the room. Sometimes that was all it took for him to climb back into his sulky shell I was working so hard to get him out of.

"Hey, Uncle Derek. Holly and I cooked dinner," Sam said brightly, and I let out an audible sigh of relief.

"Wow, I wasn't sure Holly even knew how to cook," Derek replied. Sam and I looked at each other and laughed at our inside joke. Derek didn't seem to mind that he wasn't in on it. I think he was glad Sam was laughing.

"Sam, will you go upstairs and bring down that newspaper clipping we found today?" I asked, referring to the one with the picture of Graham.

"Sure," Sam answered and dutifully went upstairs to retrieve it.

Derek walked farther into the kitchen. I was standing in front of the stove stirring the pot of pasta that was boiling. He came up behind me to get a better look at what I was making.

"And you can cook too," he said.

It seemed like a common thing someone might say, but when he spoke those words, it was like a switch flipped and I was no longer in control of my body. The next thing I knew, Derek pushed me up against the countertop next to the stove while his lips searched for mine. He cupped my face with his hands, and I put my hands on his hips to steady myself. The insatiable hunger in his kiss made my body push closer to his. He slowed the kiss and pulled away ever so slightly making me sway toward him wanting more. He leaned in again and teased the inside of my lips with his tongue. My hands slid up to his chest and I could feel his racing heart beneath my palms. I let out a soft moan and he deepened the kiss. We stayed that way with our hands roaming each other's bodies when suddenly we split apart as if a lightning bolt had struck us.

We stood staring at each other for a moment, not speaking, trying to regain our senses.

"I got the article you wanted Holly," Sam announced. I looked at him as he walked back into the kitchen, breaking the trance Derek and I were in. Afraid to look back at Derek, I thanked Sam and quickly turned back to the stove and resumed stirring the pasta.

"Hey, what do you have there, buddy?" Derek asked, trying to sound interested instead of nervous and guilty.

Thankfully Sam didn't pick up on Derek's voice and proceeded to show Derek the clipping with the photo of his grandfather.

"Ah yes, this picture," Derek said as he took the clipping from Sam to examine it. "My parents have this picture framed on the wall of their den. This is grandpa Graham's official sheriff's photo."

It occurred to me then that Celia was not the only one who lost her world that day. Derek's father and uncle, Graham's boys, were orphaned when he died since their mother had died months earlier in childbirth with Derek's father.

"What happened to your dad and uncle after this accident?" I asked, looking over Derek's shoulder to see the picture again. From reading Celia's journal, I knew that Paul was three-years old, and Thomas not yet a year old.

"Their mother's parents took them in," he said. "I don't know much more than that. They were both old by the time I was born. My dad helped take care of them, but they were in a nursing home, so my brother and I only visited them on holidays."

I somehow hoped that Derek's father would know something more about Celia or the plan that she was to be their stepmother, but he was just a baby, and his uncle not old enough to remember either. I doubted that they were even aware that their father was going to marry someone else. I wondered if their grandparents on their mother's side knew either. I felt sad that Celia seemed to be a big secret to everyone. Even if they had known about her, I wondered if they would have let her be a part of their lives. She had no real ties to them as she hadn't yet married their father. On the day of Graham's accident she lost two children as well. Two children so young that if everything worked out as planned, Celia would have been the only mother they ever knew.

I shook off this feeling of sadness and loss and walked back to the stove announcing, "Dinner is ready."

Finding a place to eat dinner presented a challenge. The house was a shambles as Ned and Charlie and a few men who they employed moved furniture around so that it was out of the way of the impending construction that, to my joy, was going to start the next day. Unfortunately, that meant that there was no dining table for us to eat dinner on. Our solution was to eat around the coffee table located in the future sitting room area. We pulled a couch and chair into the room and set up a small living space.

In the tiny kitchen, the three of us managed to fit and became an assembly line. Derek, as the tallest member, got plates out of the high cabinet and handed them one by one to Sam who placed them on the countertop for me to fill them. Sam also got napkins and knives and forks and placed them on the coffee table as it awaited the dishes. As I filled the plates with pesto chicken and spaghetti with garlic knots, I handed them back to Sam and he set them on the table.

The three of us got our drinks and marched together into our makeshift living room/dining room area. Sam took the chair, leaving the sofa for Derek and me to share. I had a twinge of guilt about eating off Celia's antique coffee table, so I scurried back into the kitchen to retrieve placemats that I had discovered while looking for utensils, and three coasters for our drinks. Derek looked somewhat relieved to have cover for the priceless table as well and Sam obligingly used them although undoubtedly not aware of the potential value of this table.

As we ate, we talked about our day. Sam and I did most of the talking about the treasures we found in our cleanup. Derek listened but was quiet about his day. The boys must have enjoyed the food because they ate every bit and went back for seconds.

Once we were finished and the dishes were in the sink, Derek announced, "I have a surprise for you two."

Sam perked up with wonder. "What is it?" he asked.

"Come outside and help me get it out of my truck. Okay, Sam?" Derek asked. Sam was out the front door almost before Derek finished asking the question. I went back into the kitchen to start washing dishes.

Moments later, Derek and Sam emerged through the front door carrying a large flat-screen TV, which they placed on top of the remaining cabinet that enclosed the circle of our thrown together sitting area.

"I know that this doesn't really go with the antique look you've got going in here, but I noticed you didn't have a TV so I wondered how we would watch the Revengers," Derek pronounced.

"It's the Avengers," Sam and I corrected in unison.

Derek smiled. "See, we need this. I have so much to learn," he said in fake defeat.

"Thank you," I said. "And by the way, you have just put that TV on top of the TV."

They looked confused. I walked over to the cabinet and opened the two doors which revealed a TV.

"It was common for people to hide their TVs in furniture back when this house was decorated. Personally, I can't understand the TV not being the focal point of the room. Also, this TV is broken," I said, pointing to the old one in the cabinet. "So, thank you for this, but another problem is that there isn't exactly a WiFi connection in here."

"No problem," Derek reassured. "I've got this."

Derek went to work setting up the TV as I washed the dinner dishes and Sam dried. If I had just been wearing a dress and pearls, we could have been something out of a 1950's TV show ourselves. I was not sure I liked it. I thought I would have to change the vibe in this house in some way.

"Got it!" Derek announced as he got the picture to come on the screen.

"Great," I praised. "How did you do it?"

"Amazon prime, a fire stick, and…you might not like this part," he started, sounding guilty, "borrowing the internet connection from the church."

"We are stealing WiFi from a church?" I asked in muted horror.

"Father Matthew gave me the WiFi password when the town hall had a pipe burst and we had to hold the town council meeting in the church basement. Is it my fault that they never changed the password?" he asked, trying to rationalize.

"I tell you what. I will save your soul and call tomorrow to get internet set up here," I promised. "Tonight, we can use it, but I think you should make a little donation to the church tomorrow."

"Deal," Derek said, bringing up the search screen to find a movie for us to watch. "Where do we start?"

Sam and I looked at each other. "Ironman!" we said together.

"Wow," Derek said sarcastically, "Maybe the two of you hanging out every day isn't such a good idea." Then he smiled at me. I knew that smile was because he was glad that Sam had a friend. Granted I was not a friend his age, but I was there for him. Ganging up on Derek had become our favorite pastime, but I made sure that it was all in fun and that any negative feelings I had toward Derek if I even still had any, wouldn't reflect on Sam. Even though he fought it, Sam wanted Derek to love him, to be the father that he lost. And Derek, I could tell, wanted that more than anything too.

The movie started and Sam stayed on the chair leaving Derek and me on the sofa. Celia's furniture, while retro charming, was not at all comfortable. Derek and I squirmed around trying to figure out how to sit without our limbs falling asleep. We ended up with Derek sitting semi-slouched with his arm slung over the back of the sofa and me with my legs curled up beneath me, sitting sideways against the back cushion. It would have been so easy for me to tuck into the crook of Derek's arm, to lay my head against his chest, to have him wrap his arm around me. I refused to let the thought linger but my feelings wouldn't let it go.

I knew the Celia inside me was all love-struck and lusting over the Graham inside Derek, but how did I feel? I had no idea. Derek was an enigma to me. At first a crazy, irate antagonizer, then a caring, generous man who struggled to be a father figure to a child who wasn't his. On top of that, he trusted me with Sam. We didn't have the best start, but now we were getting along and coming together, dare I say, as a family? Is this what it was like for Celia and Graham? As I thought it, my heart started to flutter, and I knew it was my doing and not Celia's. I did know how I felt. I wanted to curl up in his lap. I wanted to lay my head on his shoulder. I wanted his arm around mine. I wanted Derek, but I feared if I said anything out loud it would ruin the peaceful bond we built.

"You okay?" Derek asked, looking at me and breaking into my thoughts. He tugged the back of my hair playfully and smiled.

I smiled back wondering if he was flirting with me. "Yeah, I think I'm just tired from all the work this week."

"From what I hear from Sam, you've gotten a lot accomplished."

"I'm glad I've had his help. He's a great kid."

"He really is." I sighed and tried to readjust myself on the couch.

"You sure that's all it is?"

"Well, no, I mean it has been a pretty strange week, you know?"

Derek pulled me against him and nodded while blowing out a long sigh. He knew. He definitely knew.

Chapter Eleven

*D*emolition day had arrived. Ned, Charlie and two other guys, whose names I learned were Tucker and Slim came to essentially tear apart the first floor of my house and enjoyed every minute of it. I had heard about people gutting a house and I knew what that meant – taking everything down to the studs and starting over. But when it's your house and your money it feels like they are tearing out the guts of the house as well as your own body.

Charlie could see my anxiety and brought his laptop into the kitchen where I was standing biting my nails as Slim, who was not by the way slim at all, took a sledgehammer to the middle wall.

"Hey," Charlie said loudly so that I would hear him over the noise. "Come look how pretty the house is going to look once we are done."

He turned his laptop around to show me the 3D model of the completed house that we had designed together. I took a deep breath and moved through it. When the house was finished it was going to be amazing.

He pointed out all the shiny and carefully planned features of the new and improved first floor. I looked at the laptop and then at him. He was a few years older than me and just a few inches taller. He had shaggy brown hair that hung ever so stylishly over one bright blue eye. He had just enough five o'clock shadow to look scruffy, but intentional. He always seemed to wear hoodies and jeans, and his tattoos peeked out slightly when the sleeve of his hoodie lifted from his wrist. Charlie was good looking, and he was smart. He revolutionized Ned's construction business by taking it out from the back of his hardware store and putting it in front as the real money-maker. As he moved the mouse over the 3D model of the kitchen, my heart raced. Goodbye tiny galley kitchen. Hello dream kitchen.

"You really did a great job planning what this floor would look like. Not everyone has an eye for that. You do," he complimented me.

"Thank you. I am most excited about the kitchen. I can't wait to get in here and come up with a daily menu and try new dishes…" I trailed off in my fantasy of being a chef at the bed and breakfast.

"And you can cook too," Charlie added.

I froze. Those were the exact words Derek said in the exact spot in this kitchen that triggered Celia and Graham to emerge in us and lead to that long hot kiss. *Oh no. Not now.* Not in front of Ned and Slim and whatever the hell the other guy's name was. Just not now.

I braced myself for the feelings to come but there was nothing.

The spirits that inhabited the house were not invoked. I had no uncontrollable desire to reach for Charlie. He was still and looking at me apologetically, obviously thinking he said the wrong thing. I was composed enough now to remember that the "other guy's" name was Tucker. I tried speaking to see if I could.

"Yes. I love to cook," I croaked, shocked that words were able to come out of my mouth.

Looking slightly confused at the long pause I took before answering, he offered, "Well, I love to eat so if you ever need a taste tester you can call me."

Before I could respond, the front door opened, and Derek and Sam walked in looking surprised at all the destruction. I forgot to tell them that demolition was starting early this morning. They skirted around the debris to where Charlie and I were standing in the kitchen.

"Hey Buddy," I yelled at Sam over the noise, "why don't you just go upstairs, and I will meet you up there in a few minutes." Sam nodded, glad to get out of the way and ran up the stairs.

Derek tried to just give me a wave and dash, but I wanted to talk to him. I excused myself from Charlie and followed Derek out the door. It had been so loud in there that he hadn't realized that I was following him. As we reached his truck, I called his name and startled him.

"Holly, sorry I didn't know you were coming out with me," he explained, trying to regain his masculine composure. "Everything okay?"

"Something happened," I started. "I was standing in the kitchen with Charlie like you and I were last night, and Charlie said that exact phrase you said that got Celia and Graham going."

"So, did it happen again with…Charlie?" he asked. I couldn't read his expression. Was it concern? Curiosity? Jealousy?

"No, that's just it. It was the same scenario, and nothing happened," I emphasized the *nothing happened* part. I'm not sure why though. To express that it was different or to reassure Derek? Maybe both.

"Oh," Derek said, releasing the breath he must have been holding. "That's good. I mean that's interesting."

"What do you think that means? That it only works between you and me?" I asked him like there was a handbook for being possessed by your sex crazed dead relatives and he was ahead on the reading.

"Maybe it's just Celia who's haunting the house and she likes me because I look a little like my grandfather," he offered seriously. I mean that was as plausible as any other theory.

We both looked at each other and the contemplative expressions we were both wearing like we had an actual chance of figuring this out.

"What are we ghost psychologists now?" I asked and we started to laugh. Snickering at first and then full on pee-your-pants hysterical laughter. We laughed like that for at least five minutes, right there on the street in front of his truck. Neighbors must have thought we were crazy. We thought we were crazy so why not?

Calming his laugher and wiping the tears from his eyes, Derek confessed, "I was thinking about going inside and punching Charlie in the face for stealing my place as Graham's vessel and kissing you... I mean Celia."

I stopped laughing. He was jealous. But of what part? Unless he was joking. "Can you imagine having to explain that to the police after he had you arrested for assault?" I asked, pretending I hadn't read anything personal in his statement.

He clicked his door lock and partially opened it. "That would be an interesting conversation with Sheriff Wilcox," he answered still smiling. "Hey so we obviously aren't going to be able to eat dinner there for a while. Why don't you come hang out with me and Sam at our house tonight? I can cook dinner for you."

"Well okay. Thanks," I answered, surprised by the invitation.

"Oh, and my dad is coming over tonight too," he threw in as he got into the truck and started it like it was no big deal.

The rest of the day progressed like I was in a timewarp. At first it felt like the day would never end and Sam and I would never get out of the one bedroom we had been working on but when I would check on the demolition progress, I was shocked by how much they had done. During one of my breaks, Slim let me take a whack at a wall with the sledgehammer. Talk about a stress release, no wonder Slim seemed so even-keeled.

By 4 p.m. the demo crew had quit for the day leaving the previously dingy but livable first floor in utter wreckage. My heart lurched when I came down to look at it just before they left the house. *Celia, I am so sorry. What have I done to your house?*

As though reading my mind, Ned walked over to me pausing from collecting his lunchbox, water bottle and tools. "It looks bad now," he said. "but once we start rebuilding it's going to be amazing. I promise." He gave my elbow a reassuring squeeze and walked back to retrieve his things before walking out the door.

I sighed, hoping he was right.

"Holly, come look at this," Sam hollered down the stairs to me. I figured there was some other trinket or outdated gadget he found that needed explanation. Previous items he was baffled by were a record player, a rotary phone and a powder puff.

I was glad to go back upstairs. The state of the first floor was making me sad.

When I reached the top of the steps, I turned to enter the bedroom we had been working in all day. "Sam?" I called, not seeing him in the room. That didn't mean he wasn't in there. The mounds of donation items and walls of trash bags we filled blocked most of the room.

"Holly, in here!" Sam called from another bedroom we hadn't explored yet. I followed his voice and walked down the hall to one of the smaller rooms. The door was partially open.

"Did you get bored with the first room?" I asked, understanding completely if he had. We were just about finished in there anyway.

Pushing the door opened farther, I entered and stood next to Sam whose expression was that of an explorer who just found a new cave full of ancient hieroglyphics. I scanned the room taking it all in with confusion and disbelief. It was a child's room which was not the unexpected part because obviously Graham's children would need a room or two of their own. It was the fact that the room was clutter-free and perfectly preserved. It was decorated in a way typical of the 1940's. Like the rest of the house it did show signs of age. The peeling wallpaper had a peach background that featured a pattern of cartoon like characters. There was a blonde-haired mother hanging laundry on a clothes line, a brunette mother washing clothes in a tub while pointing a finger at her baby sitting on a blanket in front of her, a house, a cat, a dog and a crib in a repeating pattern lining the entire room. There was a toy chest overflowing with toys including a stuffed teddy bear. The furniture was cherry wood like the rest of the house. A dresser was pushed up against the wall. It was clearly not just a child's room, but the nursery. I realized that this would have been Derek's father's room had everything worked out. There was a sadness in the perfectness of this room. Like a mother without a baby.

Moving my eyes from the walls of the room inward, I made another shocking observation: there were two cribs.

I gasped and covered my mouth with my hand as I tried to piece everything together. How old had Derek's uncle been again when Graham had died? My mind raced to find the answer from what I read in the journals. *Three.* Would a three-year-old still be sleeping in a crib? *Maybe.* I tried to comfort myself, but I had to see something else. I darted out of the room.

Sam called out to me, "Holly, what's wrong? What are you doing?"

I went to the bedroom next to this one and took a deep breath before turning the doorknob. I didn't really pay attention to the details of the room when I first went through them all. If it was just another bedroom with overstated floral wallpaper and a full-size bed it meant nothing. It wasn't. It was painted navy blue with accents of red and white. The carpet was a faded dark blue as well. Pushed up against the wall was a twin bed with a blue and white-striped blanket neatly tucked in around the mattress military style. In the corner was a Red Radio Flyer wagon. Its passengers were stuffed animals including a teddy bear that matched the one in the nursery. This was to be three-year-old Paul's room. So, who was the additional crib in the nursery for?

I had stopped reading Celia's journals after the time Derek and I read them together. Things had gotten busy and as much as I was curious about Celia's life, I had my own to attend to – including learning how to set up and run a bed and breakfast. I decided at that moment more reading was necessary to find out about that extra crib. I hoped that it was not for the reason I suspected.

Sam joined me in the child's bedroom. "Did she have kids?" he wondered aloud to me. Two minutes ago, I was sure the answer to that question was no, but now I was not so sure.

"Wow, it's getting late. Derek will be here soon. I'd better change my clothes," I said, changing the subject and walking into the room I had been using as a bedroom. I told Sam he could go downstairs and watch TV if he wanted to.

What do you wear to meet the father of the guy you aren't dating who is possessed by his father and occasionally makes out with the women who would have been his stepmother as she inhabits your body? *A sundress. You wear a sundress.*

I was covered in grime to the point it felt like it had settled into my pours, so I decided to take a quick shower before changing. After showering, I pulled my favorite red sleeveless sundress out of the closet. It had a giant floral pattern much like most of the wallpaper in the house. I put the dress on and twirled. Who says red heads can't wear red? I dried my hair and applied my makeup finishing with bright red lips. I stepped into black wedge strappy sandals and was ready to go.

I heard Derek fly through the front door and call for Sam. Perfect timing. When I got to the top of the stairs, Sam had turned off the TV and was standing next to Derek. They both looked up when they saw me. I noticed Derek's mouth drop open and Sam blushed a little and tried to hide a smile. *Hmmm, guess this dress still has it.*

Just before I reached the bottom, Derek approached me and took my hand to escort me the rest of the way down the stairs. I worried that such a gentlemanly gesture might have been something his grandfather would have done thus invoking our uninvited spirits. Luckily, it didn't.

"Wow, Holly, you look so beautiful," Derek said, holding onto my hand a little while after I was safely down the stairs.

"Thank you," I said, trying not to blush and failing. "Everyone hungry for dinner? I can hardly wait to see what Derek is preparing for us."

Sam nodded and raced out to Derek's truck. I turned toward my car and Derek stopped me. "You can ride with us. I can drive you home later," he offered. I agreed and got into the passenger side and Sam got in the backseat.

I wasn't sure what I expected Derek's house to look like, but a single-family rancher wasn't it. As we turned into his driveway, I took in the brick house and its perfectly landscaped yard. There were azalea bushes under the window, a large cherry tree in the middle of the yard and meticulously cut grass.

Derek's father was in the driveway when we pulled in. I wasn't sure why, but I felt nervous to meet him. Sam was deliriously happy to see his grandfather and barely waited for Derek to stop the truck before jumping out to greet him.

I was about to open the truck door when I felt the ease of someone pulling it open from the other side. Derek's father was opening the door for me. I smiled at the gesture and stepped out of the car.

"Well, you must be Holly," he stated once I was standing fully upright in front of him. "I've heard a lot about you from Sam … and Derek." He winked at me. What did that mean? What had Derek told him about me? There was potential that what he said could have been bad. At least I knew he didn't tell him I was some old lady living in the house like Sam tried to get me to believe when we first met. Five minutes in and it was already going to be an interesting night.

We all walked up the path to the front door of the house together. Sam was chatting his grandfather's ear off about the superhero comics he was reading as we reached the door. Derek unlocked it and we all entered.

The best way to describe the style of Derek's house would be sophisticated man cave. The front door opened to his living room. I noticed the floors first mostly because I was looking down so I wouldn't trip on the sandals I hadn't worn in some time. The floors were hardwood with an area rug of browns and navy blues over top. A leather sofa was against the wall to the right, a heavy wood coffee table in front and two matching leather chairs to the side. Behind the sofa was a print of a map of Europe that covered most of the wall. The other walls were painted a dark navy blue and across the room was a fireplace with an enormous TV mounted above it with a built-in bookcase full of books flanking each side. It was almost exactly what I wanted to do in the sitting area of my bed and breakfast. I considered taking a picture of it for Ned and Charlie, but then thought better of it.

Derek asked us to sit in the living room as he went around the corner to the kitchen. Sam, using all his manners, asked his grandfather and me if we would like a drink.

"You know what I like," Sam's grandfather answered. "And bring one for Holly too." I was intrigued. Did he seem like a beer guy, or maybe whiskey, or perhaps Manhattans were his drink of choice? I hoped it was not a Manhattan. I remember my own grandfather drinking those and sneaking a sip to discover they tasted like lighter fluid. I didn't think I could pretend to like that even just to be polite.

"So, Mr. Sterling," I started, making small talk, "what kind of a chef is Derek - should I be worried?"

He laughed. "First, please call me Thomas," he said. "If he's making chicken, we're okay."

"I am making chicken!" Derek shouted from the kitchen obviously overhearing the conversation.

I giggled and Sam appeared from the kitchen with two large glasses of white wine. I was happy that Thomas was a wine drinker. I took a sip and smiled. He looked pleased that I liked his choice. Our conversation continued as Derek prepared our dinner. I was relieved that he was easy to talk to.

"Holly, I hear you are fixing up Miss Celia's house," Thomas said. "I wasn't aware that she had any relatives. I'm sorry for your loss."

Uh oh, I thought. Was this going to be a setup for him to claim birthright to the house? I felt like I should be cautious in my answer. "She was my great-aunt, my grandmother's sister. We would visit her occasionally at her house. I was surprised that she left it to me. I immediately thought of turning it into a bed and breakfast."

"This town could use a bed and breakfast," he replied the same as anyone who heard of my plan had said. It was comical now.

"Dad, come on," Derek scolded as he came out from the kitchen to join us. "Dinner is ready."

We got up from the living room carrying our wine glasses with us. I nudged Sam who was sitting on the floor wearing headphones so he could quietly play a video game. He took the headphones off and followed behind us through the kitchen to the connecting dining room.

The dining room housed a heavy wood table much like the coffee table in the living room. The wall was painted a dark toffee color that complimented the hardwood floors. The dining chairs were upholstered in brown, navy and ivory striped material and the walls were covered with more maps. I looked over at Sam who was dwarfed by the oversized furniture. It was apparent that Derek had decorated as a bachelor not expecting to raise a child here.

The food was plated already. There was a seasoned chicken breast accompanied by steamed vegetables. It was presented beautifully, and I was eager to see how it tasted. I picked up my fork to take a bite just as Thomas spoke.

"Come on what?" he said to Derek, bringing not only the wine, but the conversation in from the living room.

Derek looked at me and then down at his plate not wanting to go wherever he thought this conversation was taking us.

I chimed in. "Thomas, did you know my aunt?" I watched Derek tense.

"I knew her a little. I was born in Friendsville. My mother and father both passed when I was a baby though, so I went to live with my maternal grandparents a few towns over. My grandparents would bring my brother and me back here when we were children for special events like parades or the Christmas tree lighting. My grandparents on my father's side still lived here too. So, we would visit them as well. As you have found out by now, everybody knows everybody in this town. I remember Miss Celia always being kind to my brother and me. She would bring us candy when she saw that we were in town. I didn't see much of her as I grew up though. She seemed to mostly keep to herself in that house."

"The house your father bought?" I said. We might as well talk about the elephant in the room.

He calmly took a sip of his wine. "That was an old family legend. No one ever had proof that he owned that house." Thomas said, setting his glass down to try his chicken.

WAIT. WHAT? From Celia's journals I knew, unless she was mistaken, that he bought the house. I was surprised Derek's own father didn't believe the house was rightfully theirs.

Derek choked on his chicken. I feel like he knew that statement was coming, but it took him by surprise anyway. I shot a glaring look at him.

"Can we please change the subject? We don't need to talk about sensitive family business," Derek said once he was able to speak again. I thought that was directed to Thomas at first and so did Thomas because he raised a hand as though to surrender.

But then I felt Derek looking at me. It was me who he didn't want to talk about family business because from reading Celia's journals I knew more about Thomas' father than he did. I could have easily blurted out the fact that Celia was nearly his stepmother and that his father was in love with her without thinking. I felt ashamed and I hadn't even done anything wrong, but that was not the kind of thing you should find out about your father in the middle of a casual dinner. I could have casily slipped and told him something I shouldn't have. I was grateful for Derek's reminder, but the tone of the delivery could have used some work though.

"Sam, why don't you tell your grandfather all the cool old things we've been finding in the house," I redirected.

Derek looked at me and mouthed "thank you" while Sam was busy talking about record players and rotary phones. I figured Thomas would get a kick out of the fact that Sam thought of them as ancient artifacts instead of everyday household items. I relaxed and thought I might have just taken how Derek spoke too personally. He was trying to protect his father.

When we finished dinner, which turned out to be delicious, Derek scooped up our clean plates and took them into the kitchen. I grabbed mine and Sam's and followed Derek to the sink. The kitchen was small but functional. All the appliances were stainless steel and the countertops marble above and below dark wood cabinets. I helped Derek load the dishwasher – jealous that he didn't have to hand wash everything – and then got plates out of the cabinet at his request for dessert. He pointed to a chocolate cake on the counter that would be our dessert. I was impressed by his dinner and wondered how he had pulled it together.

"Dinner was delicious," I complimented, "And this cake … wow."

Derek smiled a knowing smile and said, "Thanks. I will share my secret." He got close to me and I could smell the faded scent of his cologne which I unintentionally breathed in remembering each time he had gotten close to me. "Instant pot," he said.

I laughed, broken away from the allure of his scent. "Really? I wanted to get one of those but honestly I'm too afraid to try it," I confessed. "And the cake?"

"Dotty," he whispered like I thought he had baked it himself and would be disappointed by the truth. "She is a professionally trained pastry chef."

I was impressed. It seemed like everyone in this town had a secret. My mind went to the nursery that Sam and I had discovered earlier in the day and the two cribs. I wondered what other secrets my aunt had kept all those years. I would have to tell Derek about our discovery, but not yet. Now it was time for cake.

I sliced four pieces out of the enormous cake and plated them with a fork. Derek took them out to the dining room and asked his father if he wanted coffee. "Just decaf if you have it," Thomas answered, "Otherwise I'll never sleep tonight."

Derek obliged, offering decaf coffee to me too which I accepted, and a glass of chocolate milk for Sam. Thomas told hilarious stories through dessert about trips he had been on, things he and his friends had done in their youth and stories about Derek's mother that for woman solidarity sake alone I wasn't sure I should have laughed at. He was a delightful man and obviously adored Derek's mother.

Looking at the clock which read 9:06 p.m., and then at Sam who was falling asleep in his chair, Derek said, "Hey Sam, why don't you head to bed?"

Sam agreed without resistance and sleepily hugged his grandfather and high-fived Derek. Then he came over to me and gave me a bear hug as big as his sleepy self could muster. He said good night to everyone and headed down the hall to bed.

"Dad, are you driving home tonight or staying?" Derek asked.

"Well your mom is at her girls scrapbooking retreat this weekend, so she won't be home until tomorrow night. Okay if I stay?" he asked.

"Of course, and then you can have more wine," Derek offered. Thomas nodded in agreement to that too. Derek got up and checked on Sam, coming back a few minutes later to rejoin us at the table.

We stayed at the table and chatted a little longer. Thomas had another glass of wine and then declared that it was time for bed. He hugged Derek and kissed me on the top of the head.

"It was lovely to meet you Holly. I hope to see you again." With that he shuffled down the hall to the guest bedroom leaving Derek and me alone.

"I can take you home now if you want," he started and then hesitantly added, "or we could go back in the living room and talk for a while."

"Maybe you should just take me home now," I decided. Derek nodded looking a little disappointed, but he got up from his chair and took the remaining dishes into the kitchen before retrieving his keys.

Part of me wanted to stay and cozy up on the leather sofa with him and possibly talk all night. The other part, the logical part of my brain, reminded me that it was the Celia and Graham parts of us who were in love. Holly and Derek were still at a stalemate. Nothing was resolved about the house. Even Randy was having trouble giving me legal possession of the house without the deed. Apparently, there was a fire at the town courthouse the year that the house was purchased, and the records were either lost or destroyed. He was working on a resolution, but he encouraged me to keep searching the house to try and find the document.

While Derek was in the kitchen, I asked to use the bathroom. He uttered some direction about going down the hall, but I couldn't really hear him. The house was not that big, I was sure I could find it on my own. I started down the hall and was faced with the decision of choosing between two doors. Did he say on the left or on the right? I took a shot and chose wrong. I opened the door to what must have been Derek's office. I was about to shut the door when something caught my eye.

On a table in the middle of the room was a scaled model of the town of Friendsville. I identified the bridge I drove across on my way into town and then the rest was barely recognizable. The buildings just over the bridge that I was sure were previously abandoned were replaced or maybe just converted into tourist attraction businesses. There was one for white water rafting and another for charter fishing. There was a hiking trail that led to the river. A few businesses remained the same. Dotty's Diner was still intact as was Ned's hardware store and the market, probably to keep the quaint town appeal for the tourists. Past the church was a lodge with about thirty rooms. All of this looked like a brilliant way to bring life back to the town. There was probably more that I missed, but I didn't want to get caught snooping. Before I left the room to find the bathroom, I looked at the model one more time and had a disturbing realization. Next to the church, where my house currently stood, was a parking lot with the sign "Overflow Parking." Somehow, I thought Ned was kidding when he said that the house would be knocked down and made into a parking lot – like an exaggeration for effect. I was hurt and stunned.

I left the room and closed the door behind me. I crossed the hall and found the actual bathroom. When I was finished, I went back down the hall to the living room where Derek was holding his keys. I wanted to confront him with what I saw, but then he would know that I was snooping.

"Everything okay?" he asked like he could feel a shift in temperature as I went cold.

"Great," I answered curtly and headed for the door.

We drove the ten minutes back to my house in complete silence. It was weird to be angry at Derek again after all the quality time we had been spending together. I was naïve to think that he was just going to surrender and let me have the house without a fight. I blasted myself for letting my guard down with him. We were not becoming friends and especially not more than friends no matter how I felt the other night after dinner. Keep your friends close and keep your enemies closer was going through my head. That is what he must have been doing. Well two can play at that game. I was going to continue doing everything I was doing including nightly dinners and movies with Derek and Sam. I would make him feel as welcome and comfortable in the house as I possibly could. I would make him fall in love with the house as if it were his own home. I would make sure that the thought of knocking it down would be as heartbreaking to him as it was to me. How could he let me put all my money into this renovation if he still planned on taking the house from me? Who does that? One thing I knew for sure was that I would not fall in love with Derek Sterling. Maybe his charm and good looks and the fact that he smelled so good was starting to wear me down, but I wouldn't fall into that trap. Everything I did from this moment on would be intentional and calculated friendliness. I wouldn't be letting my guard down again.

"Holly?" Derek said, breaking me out of my thoughts. "We're home."

Good, I thought, please think of it as home. I nodded at him and opened my door. He turned off the engine and got out too. We stood awkwardly next to each other. I'm not sure why. We weren't coming back from a date. I didn't just meet his dad in the way that you bring your girlfriend home to meet your parents. It was dinner and a ride home. That was it. So why did this feel so weird? It was just me projecting. It had to be. Derek certainly wasn't standing there waiting to see if I wanted him to kiss me goodnight.

"I wanted to thank you," Derek began, looking down at his feet, "for taking care of Sam. For finding him that day and befriending him.

He trusts you and he doesn't trust people easily. I know he basically hates me for not being his father and I get that, but it's hard and I am trying my best." He looked up at me as he continued. "I know that you don't trust me or even like me, but I appreciate that you don't try to turn Sam against me."

I think he was waiting for me to disagree and say that I did like him, but I focused on the part about Sam. Everything I felt about Sam was genuine and only had his best interests at heart, no matter my feelings about Derek. "I would never do that," I said, touching his arm so he knew I was being sincere. "But you're right, I don't trust you." I told him with confidence I didn't know I had.

He seemed surprised at what I said. I was right that he thought I would challenge his self-deprecation and tell him he was wrong, and he shouldn't think that way. Maybe he thought I would swoon and tell him that my true heart's desire was to be with him always like some cheesy romance novel, but I didn't. I told him the truth.

He nodded his head like he was processing what I just professed and then he looked at me and spoke. "Because of the house? You don't trust me because of the house?"

I nodded. "That house is part of both of us. If things worked out the way they were headed, you probably would have spent your summers there with your grandparents, Graham and Celia. You would even have more aunts or uncles if they had children together," I said, thinking of the nursery Sam and I found earlier that day.

"Why is this house so important to you? Did you even really know your aunt? Did you even like her?" he asked.

While he wasn't wrong, the questions hit the pit of my stomach. Why was the house so important to me? Had I only started this bed and breakfast idea because people kept telling me that was what I should do? Was I just trying to stick it to this stranger who had yelled at me in the diner? Showing up the instigator who parked bulldozers on my lawn and threated to tear it down around me?

I paused for a few beats and then answered, "Because I feel connected to the house."

The truth was that I felt like I was destined to end up like Celia – a lonely bitter old lady just like one of my ex-roommates had predicted. Maybe I would end up alone, but it was going to be on my terms. I was going to do better for Celia. I was going to make her house into a place where people would come to stay and relax. Even if I ended up alone, there would always be people around me so I would never have the chance to feel lonely. That was why the house was so important to me. For the first time in my life, I was going to be brave. I was finally going to stick with something because this felt like the answer to the question I had been asking since I graduated from college. What am I going to do with my life? The answer: I am going to make a place for myself in this town and I am going to succeed in creating a business that the town needed.

"I need to go," I told him. "Construction starts early tomorrow."

"Okay," he said. "I'm taking the day off tomorrow to spend with my dad and Sam, so I won't be bringing Sam over tomorrow."

I felt my heart sink a little. It shouldn't have been a big deal. Caring for Sam was supposed to be like a job. I should have felt relieved to have the day off, but I didn't. I was sad that he wouldn't be there. Pathetic I know, but the ten-year-old boy was the best friend I had in this town.

"Oh okay," I answered, more solemnly than I had hoped. "Tell him we can try to solve the mystery of the two cribs the next time."

I dangled that piece of information in front of Derek hoping he would take the bait and ask about it. It didn't seem to register with him.

He just nodded and waved and got back into his truck. I walked up to the house alone.

Chapter Twelve

The pounding on my front door early the next morning woke me from my sound sleep. I leaped out of bed realizing the construction crew was there ready to start the day. I pulled on a silk robe that I found in one of Celia's closets which was much too fancy to be paired with my cotton shorts and tank top I wore to bed. No matter, no time. I raced to answer the door.

When I opened the door, I was greeted by Ned offering me a cup of Dotty's special coffee in a to-go cup. I took it from him gratefully. I should serve this at my bed and breakfast. I wondered if I could form a partnership with Dotty to supply coffee and pastries to my B&B. I held that idea in the back of my mind as I turned to face the rubble that was the first floor of said B&B. *There are going to be a few steps before figuring out what kind of coffee I would serve to my hypothetical guests.*

"Good morning," Ned greeted me after I had mindlessly snatched the coffee from his hand without thanking him.

"Good morning Ned," I smiled. "Thank you for the coffee."

"Looks like you needed it hon. Rough night?" he asked.

I shrugged and headed back upstairs. Catching a glimpse of myself in the mirror, I realized just why Ned had asked. My hair was piled on top of my head in a messy bun, the bags under my eyes had dark circles from the mascara I forgot to wash off before climbing into bed. I was tired. I thought that I may have been dreaming all night, but I couldn't remember any of my dreams.

I heard the rumbling, drilling, and hammering begin as I got in the shower to try to make myself feel human again. As I stood letting the water rush over me, I remembered that Sam was not coming over today. What would I do with myself?

My shower was cut short when the water abruptly turned off. Thank goodness I already washed the shampoo out of my hair. *Thanks for the warning guys.* I got out of the shower and threw on some sweats, tied my hair up in a messy bun, and took a deep breath. I walked down the hall to Celia's bedroom. I had peeked into it several times since my arrival, but today I felt like I needed to actually fill in the blanks about her life and I knew that if there was anywhere in the house that held her secrets, it was in this room.

I stepped into the room and immediately felt like I went back in time, much like the first time I stepped foot into the house. I could see what the room looked like seventy-years ago when Celia was still just a girl preparing for her happily ever after.

The wallpaper was the bright florals that she loved so much and threaded throughout the house. Navy blue with large glistening white gardenias in this room – a touch feminine and a touch masculine. It was to be a shared space of husband and wife in perfect unity. The floors were carpeted wall-to-wall in dark navy blue. There was a bed pushed up against the wall with a red, white, and blue striped duvet and fluffy pillows – a marriage bed.

The dresser was across the room. The top was covered in three clean-white crocheted doilies, a jewelry box atop the middle one, perfectly arranged bottles to the right, and a silver tray to the left that held recently worn jewelry and a man's watch. The watch must have belonged to Graham, but I couldn't imagine her just letting it sit there on the dresser after all these years. It was in perfect condition and not a speck of dust on it – a gift she had never been able to give him? It was face down, but I could hear it ticking. I stepped closer and saw that it was engraved. It read: "To the man I love, on our wedding day. Always and Forever." I felt my chest tighten with her pain. The emotion was so intense I thought I might have to grab onto the dresser to keep myself upright, but I wasn't sure if it was really even there. *Why would she keep this watch right on top of her dresser where she would have to look at it every day?* Perhaps, it served as a memory of him or maybe she felt like if she kept it there, he would return to her someday.

The closet was to the right of the dresser – a wooden door painted crisp white. Against the wall to the left of the bed was a dressing table with powders and lipstick, a hairbrush, and a large oval-shaped mirror with a chair in front. It was the kind of thing I had only seen in movies where rich women sat as they applied their makeup. I thought about Celia sitting here preparing herself for her wedding day. I stood behind the chair and looked into the mirror. The image I saw was not my own, but instead, it was Celia staring back at me. She was wearing the wedding dress I found in the trunk in the attic. It was cream, not white, with lace on the shoulders and satin-covered buttons down the back. She sat admiring herself in the mirror as a beautiful bride. Graham came up behind her and placed his hand on her shoulder. He was handsome in his new navy suit and tie. She put her hand on top of his and they knew that their love would last forever. *What was Celia trying to show me?* I still felt the heartbreak in my chest as I thought about how this day never came for Celia. Hearing stories about how bitter she was from my mother, Derek's father, and the people in town made me realize she never got over losing Graham. But now I felt it. I felt the pain and knew exactly why she ended up that way. The vibrant person she was in her youth, so bold and hopeful just shriveled up inside her after Graham died.

I took another look around the room through Celia's eyes. The room I saw was clean and clutter-free – freshly painted and decorated. It was hopeful and ready for the future that never came.

A loud bang from downstairs followed by a male voice cussing startled me. I ran to the door and called out to make sure everyone was okay. They were, but the distraction brought me back to reality and when I turned back to the room, I saw it as it was, a worn and dingy version of the vision I had seen. The vision of Celia and Graham was gone. The bed was different. I realized the one that was now in the attic was the bed that used to reside in this room. The carpet and wallpaper were faded and the paint on the closet door was peeling. The duvet on the new bed was replaced with a light pink blanket and matching sheets. The dresser was in the same spot, but it was cluttered and filled with medicine bottles and over-the-counter pain medication. The jewelry box and the watch on the silver tray remained, as did the doilies but they were yellowed and the watch, now face up, no longer worked – stopped at 9:06. The glamourous dressing table and the chair were gone and replaced by Celia's old favorite chair that used to be in the living room. A small television on top of a table sat in front of the chair and behind it was a bookshelf heavy with books that I hadn't noticed before. The room was clean but old and worn.

I wasn't sure how to begin to clean out Celia's most personal space. I got a trash bag and began with the bottles of medicine atop the dresser. I felt safe in assuming that Celia would be glad to have these removed, the final signs of old age tossed into the trash. I moved to the clutter on the floor – newspapers, and magazines that were not the treasured kind we found in the other bedroom, but more recently read and piled up. After I went through all the other meaningless things like her old lady clothes, worn linens, and bags, the room appeared bigger.

Next, I went over to the bookcase. I was interested to find out what Celia liked to read. Many of the shelves were full of steamy romance novels. I would have been shocked a few days ago, but after reading her journals and feeling the hardcore lust and desire she had for Graham I was not surprised. The rest of the shelves were stocked with classics and some mystery novels. The bottom shelf housed a full set of outdated encyclopedias. Intermixed with the random books, I saw a familiar green spine with the date 1946 handwritten vertically down the side. It was the final journal for that infamous year. It seemed to be the last journal she ever wrote in. I hadn't found any with dates later than that year in the bookcase nor the hope chest in the attic.

I felt the pressure of reading this journal and knew that many questions I had would be answered in it. I also knew that I would feel all the emotions attached to the words on the pages. I took the journal over to the side of the bed and sat on the floor with my back up against the bottom of the bed. I took a breath and opened the journal. It began on the day I dreaded reading about most – the day before Graham's accident. The last day they would be together.

December 2, 1946

The house was freezing when I woke. It snowed last night and from the windows, I could see the icicles hanging from the trees. I loved the snow. It made everything so bright and cheerful. It made me remember the days when I was a child sledding down the hill behind our house with my sister.

Graham would be coming by soon. He was taking the boys to their grandparents' house so they could care for them while he was on nightshift. Emma started a new job as a nanny for another family back home. She was the only person who knew about Graham and me moving into the new house together and that we would not need a nanny any longer as I would care for the children while Graham was at work. Graham was thoughtful in asking me to tell her of our plans early so that she would not be without a job longer than she had to be. He did not even mind when she left a month early and he had to make other arrangements.

I could not wait to let the whole world know we were married. On New Year's Eve, we were going to make it official. That was when Graham was planning to tell his late wife's parents, as well as his own. I could barely hold the secret whenever I talked to my mother and Alice. They thought that I was living in Friendsville as a nanny for a family that Emma told me about. I did not like to lie, but I was not sure that Mama and Daddy would understand about me marrying an older man with two small children. I feared they would try to change my mind and bring me home where Daddy would try to make it all go away and we would not speak of it again.

Now though, I am sure that they would be happy that Graham and I were married. I am two weeks late and certain that I am pregnant with Graham's third child. How wonderful that all three will be so close in age. I am consumed with thinking of how to decorate the nursery for two babies. One of the ladies in the church knitting group that I go to said *that she had a crib now that her son has grown out of it. I spoke up and told her that I would take it because my sister was expecting. I hated to lie in church but being pregnant with no husband around to speak of would have been a much worse truth to tell. I have already thought of the perfect names too. Vivien if it is a girl – after Vivien Leigh because Gone with the Wind is my favorite movie and Graham Jr. if it is a boy. I am going to tell Graham the news tonight and visit the doctor tomorrow to confirm. I am overjoyed.*

I stopped reading and just sat for a moment. Celia had been pregnant. Why didn't anyone in the family know? What happened to the baby? Was it a boy or a girl? If the child lived, they would be in their seventies by now. I can't imagine my grandmother not knowing. Maybe she never shared the secret if Celia put the child up for adoption. So far, reading this journal was creating more questions than answers and I hoped that reading more would provide them.

I went back to the entry and noticed that after that paragraph, the handwriting looked different – shakier and in a different color ink as though she stopped writing at this point and came back later to finish.

Graham came by two hours before his shift started to spend the whole time with me. We spent nearly all the time in bed. Making love with Graham was magical. Just before he had to leave to go to work, I made him dinner and thought I would share the baby news with him then. I lovingly prepared pork chops and potatoes with green beans. It was his favorite meal. I let him finish eating before I cheerfully announced that I was pregnant. But he did not say anything at first. He did not smile or scoop me up in his arms with sheer elation as I had expected.

He finally spoke. "Thomas is still in diapers and Paul barely out of them. I wasn't expecting to have another baby."

I am devastated. I could not hide my disappointed tears. I could not help noticing that he said he was not expecting to have another baby – not that he was not expecting to have another baby - yet. He told me that he was just shocked and that he just needed to think about what that meant. He said that he loved me and the boys more than anything else in the world and he would love this baby too. I was not sure I believed him.

He got up from the kitchen chair and walked toward the door. He grabbed his uniform hat and opened the door to leave. I yelled, "Graham, please don't leave!"

He stopped, put his hat down on the table. He came over to me and took me in his arms and kissed me in a way that made me feel loved and desired and hopeful. And then he left.

By this point, I was in tears. I could feel Celia's relief and hope at that moment. I touched my lips, almost able to feel the kiss she described in those pages, but I knew that she was never going to see him again. From reading the newspaper clipping I found I knew he would go on a call on the icy roads and that his police car would flip on the highway into some trees and that he died on impact.

I shut the journal. I couldn't read anymore. It was too painful to think about how she would write about the news of his death and how she would deal with her world crashing down around her. I stood up, wiped my eyes, and put the journal back in its slot in the bookcase. I moved on to another task, trying to shake off all the feelings.

I went to the jewelry box on top of the dresser thinking that looking at old and beautiful jewelry would make me feel happy. Her collection didn't disappoint. There were strings of pearls and lapel pins, clip earrings, and gold necklaces. When I laid out all the jewelry on the dresser, I looked at the bottom of the jewelry box. There was a folded piece of paper. I lifted it out and unfolded it carefully to see what it was.

It was the deed to the house.

Chapter Thirteen

I went downstairs to check on the progress of the renovation after changing out of my sweats and into cut off jean shorts and a fresh t-shirt and righting my messy bun into a dignified ponytail. The bones of the new rooms were going up and it started to feel like things were moving along. I was grateful to have the crew with Ned at the helm and I knew I could trust leaving them to it.

I needed to get out of the house to think about the things I had discovered today. I yelled to Ned through the hammering and drilling that I was going out for a little while. I opened the front door just as Derek and Sam were about to knock.

"Hi," I said, confused at the sight of them. I glanced at the clock. It was 9:06 a.m. – a little more than an hour later than Derek usually brought Sam by. "I'm sorry I thought you were spending the day with Thomas and Sam wasn't coming over."

Derek smiled that charming smile of his, "Turns out my mom ran out of scrapbooking supplies and wanted to come home early. We had breakfast with him and then sent him on his way."

It wasn't that I didn't want to spend the day with Sam in my charge, but I needed to get out of the house. I needed something to improve my solemn mood. The empath in me needed to heal.

"We wanted to see if you'd come with us for a picnic and swimming in the river," Sam announced, peeking his head out from behind Derek. Derek held up a picnic basket as proof.

I smiled. That was exactly what I needed, I realized. I wouldn't have imagined that Derek would be the one to offer it to me. I nodded and Sam cheered. I started out the door to join them when Derek said, "If you have a bathing suit you should wear it. There isn't anywhere to change there."

Oh, right, they did talk about swimming. I forgot that quickly. I really needed to get out of my own head. I thought about the clothes that I brought with me from my old apartment. It was everything I had there, but I still had a lot of clothes at my parents' house. It occurred to me that I did have a swimsuit. I wore it to a pool party that Darla convinced me to go to with her. It was an emerald green bikini. Darla said that it looked fabulous on me and brought out my red hair. I thought I could trust her. I doubted that she would want to be seen with some ugly chick, but then again, I always got the feeling she brought me to be the Duff (Designated Ugly Fat Friend). I was not fat, but I also didn't spend hours at the gym and cake on all the makeup like the rest of her friends. There were a lot of women at that party prancing around, trying to impress all the guys who were there. They were all drinking to excess which in my opinion prevented them from being impressive. That was never my scene – even when I was in my early twenties like Darla and the rest of her friends.

I wasn't so sure a bikini was the best thing to wear on this occasion to swim in a river, but better than sitting in wet shorts all day. I told Derek and Sam that I would just be a minute and bounded back up the stairs to my bedroom. I found the bikini and put it on under my clothes. I located a towel, a change of clothes and some sneakers to replace the flip flops I was wearing in case we ended up walking anywhere and shoving everything into a bag, I made my way back down the stairs.

Derek and Sam were waiting for me by the truck. There were rafts secured in the bed and the picnic basket was tucked into the backseat. Sam was waving at me excitedly to hurry up.

I sat in the passenger seat next to Derek with Sam in the back playing his video game with headphones on. As we rode to our destination, Derek gave me a mini tour of the town. Most of what I saw of the town was within walking distance of the house. We were going to the edge of town – the part I had only seen the day I arrived trying to find my way to the diner.

I had to admit it was difficult to just sit there making small talk and listening to Derek go on about the town when I was keeping a secret from him. I wasn't ready to tell him that I found the deed to the house and certainly not ready to tell him what it said. I took a deep breath and tried to focus on what he was telling me about the area.

As we crossed the bridge Derek said, "Below us is the Troubled River. This spot just over the bridge is the best place to swim but we should eat lunch first." *Ironic name for a river.*

I nodded as Derek parked as close to the edge of the road as he could. Sam must have felt the shift in the truck and took off his headphones to prepare to get out.

We exited the truck and brought the picnic basket with us as we descended a small hill to the river's edge. There were a few old but stable picnic tables at the bottom of the hill, a safe distance from the river. Derek put the picnic basket down and pulled the tablecloth from it. I helped him spread it over the table and then unpack the picnic basket. I was curious about what he packed us for lunch. He brought sandwiches, pickles, and chips from Dotty's with her famous brownies for dessert. I was amused to find three sandwiches meaning they were sure I was going to say yes to the adventure or maybe they thought they would just split it between them if I didn't.

"It's so beautiful here," I said after taking the bench facing the river.

It was a breathtaking view. The river was calm, but still moving. I wasn't sure I was up for swimming but a lazy float in a raft down the river was exactly what I needed. There were a few other rafters already in the water. They waved as they drifted past us.

"This is my favorite place in the whole world," Derek stated after finishing a bite of his sandwich.

We all just sat eating our lunch, not speaking after his declaration. We just looked out to the river, memorized by its motion. The bank of the river was wooded – a small forest on each side. The picnic area was the only clearing and was flanked by tall trees, their leaves green for the season.

"Can we get in?" Sam asked excitedly. I noticed that he devoured his lunch as though he didn't want to waste a minute getting into the river.

"I think you have to wait an hour after eating before you can get in the water or you'll get a cramp," Derek said, blankly looking at Sam for his reaction. Sam's reaction was that of horror.

"I don't think that's true," I said.

"I know. It just seemed like the proper parent thing to say at this moment," Derek replied, laughing. Sam looked relieved. I just laughed and shook my head.

Derek and I finished our lunches, deciding to save the brownies for later. We walked back up to the truck. On the way, a tree on the edge of the wooded area caught my eye. I grabbed Derek's arm to stop him from walking and pointed to it, silently.

GS + CA inside a heart was carved in the tree.

Derek smiled. "It seems like everywhere we go Graham and Celia have already been there together." He took my hand to help me back up the hill. It was a sweet and unexpected gesture. I considered pulling my hand away, but I decided that I didn't mind the assistance up the hill.

Once we reached his truck, we put the picnic basket in the backseat again. Sam impatiently helped me as I struggled to free the rafts from the truck. I was apparently the only one planning to use one. Derek and Sam told me they were going to swim, but Derek took the raft from me and carried it back down the hill.

We once again claimed the picnic table as a place to discard our extra clothing. Sam took off his shirt and shoes and, not able to contain himself anymore, ran into the river.

"Sunscreen!" Derek called out to him but then swatted at the air knowing his advice was falling on deaf ears.

Like Sam, the shorts Derek was wearing were swim trunks. He took off his shoes and placed them on the bench of the picnic table. Then he took off his shirt. I held my breath as I watched him pull the shirt over his head by the collar in one swift motion. I couldn't help noticing how muscular he was. His broad shoulders and six pack abs with evenly bronzed skin caught me off guard. I saw him without his shirt before, but at the time I must have seen him through Celia's eyes as Graham and didn't pay much attention to Derek's actual form. My mouth was suddenly dry, and I licked my lips which Derek caught me doing and smiled a crooked smile at me.

"Okay, your turn," he teased. I was suddenly shy. I hadn't worn the bikini that was hiding under my clothes since that party which may have been two summers ago, and in my rush to get out the door I didn't stop to check a mirror to see what I looked like in it. There was a time when I was a runner and had an athletic hard body, but those days were long gone. Now I had the scrawny body of a woman who couldn't settle on a job and had to choose rent, over food more times than she would like to admit. On top of that, my naturally pale skin hadn't seen the sun much less gone to the beach with any regularity.

Derek could see that I was obviously uncomfortable. "I'm just kidding," he said. "Come in when you're ready. I'm going to catch up with Sam." With that he darted off toward the river leaving me to strip down to my emerald green bikini without an audience. I was grateful.

I quickly sprayed myself with the sunscreen that Derek had offered Sam. I knew that if I didn't use it, tomorrow I would be a lobster in pain. Then I grabbed the raft and used it as a shield covering my body until I reached the water. Shoving it into the river, I most ungracefully heaved myself on to it nearly falling off twice before finally balancing myself in the middle. The sun warmed my skin and gave me a sense of peace – maybe it was just the extra vitamin D I was lacking. I watched as Derek and Sam splashed each other. The joy in Sam's laughter as he horsed around with his uncle made me so happy.

The day was perfect, and I was at ease. So much at ease, I closed my eyes to help me further relax. Drifting mindlessly in the river I thought about nothing. I was focused on the sun and the cool water my feet dangled into. I thought I could stay like this forever.

I was breathing in the fresh air when I felt cold water rush into my float and hit the middle of my bare back. I was jolted at the chill and my eyes flew open. The raft was rocking back and forth violently. Had I drifted farther down the river than I realized – into the white water I had seen when I crossed the bridge the first time I came to town? I regained my bearings and realized I was only feet from where I had entered the river. I looked to the right and saw Sam splashing in the water with some kids his own age. He looked over and started laughing. That was the moment I realized Derek was trying to knock me off my raft.

"It's time for a swim," Derek teased. "I hope you don't mind getting your hair wet!"

Before I could shout "No!" Derek rocked the float harder until ultimately it flipped, tossing me into the water and landing on top of me. I stood quickly from the shock of the cold water even though the water came up to my shoulders and it only spared that much of my skin from the cold water. The raft was on top of my head and as I cleared the water out of my eyes, I saw Derek emerge from under the water to join me underneath the float.

"You jerk!" I yelled though it was muffled in the curve of the plastic float above me. Something in that scene must have been reminiscent of a time Celia and Graham spent together because it triggered them.

Derek pulled me close to him under the cover of the raft. He looked at me for a beat and then pressed his lips to mine parting them with his tongue searching for mine. I sighed opening my mouth slightly which just deepened the kiss. I felt the hunger and the longing I had felt each time before, but there was a newness to this kiss like it was a first. Maybe Celia and Graham kissed for the first time in this very spot. No, I knew that wasn't true. They kissed for the first time the day after they met at his house. This must have been something else. The initials carved into the tree we found proved they had been here. Maybe that was the mark of some other special occasion.

I cleared my mind of wonder and put my arms around Derek's neck.

He moved his hands against the bare skin of my sides and back like he was trying to memorize my body. His touch made my skin feel warm under the cold water. As his kisses became more intense and urgent, I wanted to wrap my body around his but the air under the raft was hot and stifling. I thought for a moment I could suffocate in his arms and not care if that meant not having to ever stop touching him. And then it stopped. Derek pulled away from me with a gasp, flipping the raft off us to get some necessary air.

With us free of the raft and each other we breathed heavily both from the kiss and lack of oxygen. Our bodies were still close to each other though no longer touching. I could still feel a lingering pull between us. I swam backward a little to get farther away from him. Something was different about that encounter. I remembered everything about it. I felt and saw Derek, not the way I had before through Celia's eyes seeing Graham.

"I'm sorry," I said, not really knowing what I was sorry for. "I didn't think I could trigger them outside of the house."

"Maybe it wasn't … you," he drew out the "you" like it was not the original thing he was going to say. "I mean it could have been because I flipped you out of the float."

"Right," I agreed. "It could have been anything." I didn't know what to do next. Should I swim over to Sam or get back on the float?

Derek found my arm under the water and pulled me a little closer to him. "Do you want to leave?" he asked in a whisper, still holding my arm.

"No," I answered. "Look at Sam over there. He's having fun and making friends. We should stay."

"Okay," he agreed with a smile and let go of my arm and moved away. For a moment I felt like I was lost in the water flailing like I needed him to come back to me. Then he did, bringing my float back for me.

"Here, I promise not to dump you off it again."

I smiled and was horrified that he was holding the raft so I could get on. No one is ever graceful when getting on a raft especially from in the water. It is every person's right to struggle and look ridiculous getting back on a raft on their own without being watched. This was no time to be a gentleman. The gentlemanly thing would have been to swim to the other side pretending not to laugh at my struggle. But he didn't. He held it for each of the three attempts it took me to jump back on, my skin getting raw from the wet plastic. I tried to shimmy against it to fix my position. When I finally got back on and centered, I realized that his hand was resting on my stomach trying to help stabilize me and I felt a jolt of electricity. He moved it quickly like he felt it too. Maybe the water conducted a spiritual current of some kind. He awkwardly apologized and swam off to see what Sam was doing. We managed to avoid each other for the rest of the afternoon until it was time to get back in the truck to go home. This time Sam carried my raft to the truck. I veered off to take a closer look at that tree with the carving. I traced each letter including the heart with my fingertip. Tears welled up in my eyes thinking of the day they carved this and how happy they were planning a beautiful future together. All of it lost. It was such a bittersweet love story.

Derek rested his hand on my shoulder before moving it down my arm and grabbing mine. He could see my tears and squeezed my hand before leading me back up the hill to the truck. Once again, I let him. So much for getting away from the house and the ghosts it held there. I needed to rid myself of these spirits, these emotions that they stirred in me that were not even mine. I needed to finish whatever unfinished business Celia left. I needed to finish the house, finish the journals, finish the story.

Chapter Fourteen

December 3, 1946

I am devasted. I can't believe any of this is real.

I woke this morning and thought it was going to be like any other day. I got up, got dressed, did some things around the house, and then walked the icy sidewalks to the market to pick up some groceries around 9 a.m. As I shopped the aisles, I heard a woman and Mr. McFarland talking at the counter.

They were talking about a tragic accident that happened the night before. About what those poor babies would do now that they were orphans. About how the county had been a better place with him running the police department. About how he was always kind and friendly. My heart rose into my throat. Please, please do not be talking about Graham, I thought.

I put my basket down on the floor of the aisle and walked closer to the front trying to find out who they were talking about. Like he was trying to include me in the conversation, Mr. McFarland handed me a copy of the newspaper. It was folded to the article that read "Sheriff killed on icy highway" and there was a picture of my Graham. I paid for the newspaper and rushed out of the store before I started to cry. I left the market without any groceries. I ran home nearly sliding to the house on the ice.

Graham is dead.

December 4, 1946

My eyes are so swollen from crying for the last two days straight that I can barely see the words I am writing on the page.

I realized a hard truth too. I was Graham's dirty little secret. No one knew about our relationship so much to the point that no one knew to even tell me personally about his death. I am not going to be invited to his funeral much less plan it as a wife would. He convinced me not to tell my own family about our plan. As far as my parents and Alice knew I was living here as a nanny for a man who recently lost his wife. The town thought I was fixing up the house while I waited for my husband, who was serving overseas, to join me here in a few months. How could I be so naïve?

I should have figured it out at least when I told him I was pregnant, and he reacted so disappointedly. Funny, it turns out that I am not pregnant – my monthly visitor arrived this morning.

Graham, how could you leave me like this? What am I supposed to do now without you? I don't have a job and this house is not even mine. Where will I live? Damn you Graham Sterling for leaving me. Damn you for making me fall in love with you.

December 20, 1946

The town is decorated for Christmas. There are red and green decorations as far as the eye can see. The Christmas tree lighting was last night. I don't leave the house much these days except to go to work at the school and the market on Saturdays as early as I can, so I have less of a chance of running into nosey neighbors. But I went to the ceremony last night. I could not deny myself that. Christmas was always my favorite season. This year I will spend it alone. I am sad and ashamed that I kept Graham a secret from my family, but I am not ready to share it with them even now. I want to spend this Christmas in our house and think of him.

I saw Thomas and Paul at the tree lighting ceremony with both sets of grandparents. Paul was excitedly dancing around, and Thomas was squealing from his stroller – he has gotten so chubby. I don't know what possessed me, but I walked over to them and said hello to the grandparents and offered Paul a candy cane which he grabbed out of my hand gleefully. One of his grandmothers told him to thank the nice lady. I smiled and walked away quickly and back to the house. To those boys, I would only ever be "the nice lady" instead of their mother. I felt heartbroken all over again.

I walked back to the house just after the tree was lit. It was such a beautiful sight. I thought of how Graham and I and the boys would have been here together tonight. Paul would probably have been sitting on Graham's shoulders and I would have held Thomas in my arms comforting him so the cheering crowd didn't startle him. Maybe we would not have been there together this year. Our wedding was still eleven days away and we decided not to be seen together until after we told everyone we were married. Instead of embracing our love and showing it to the world, we hid in the shadows for fear of what others might think. It was such a waste of precious time.

Everywhere I went in town held the potential for what might have been. At the market, I dreamed of the children shopping with me and asking for candy which I would pretend I did not want them to have but then give in just as we were about to leave. Looking at the river from the bridge, I pictured all of us having a picnic together and the boys splashing around in the water while Graham held me against him, watching our family. Church and the school were the only places where I felt comfortable still attending. I had established a place at the church for myself while I was waiting for Graham and my faith was all I had to help me through this tragic season. I stopped attending the women's groups, however. I did not want to keep answering questions about when my husband would join me in town. The job I had at the school as the office clerk was fulfilling and necessary for me to support myself now. Sometimes I did let myself think about all of us sitting in church together and knew that I was now working at the school where the boys would have attended had everything worked out the way it was headed. There were so many unfulfilled dreams for me in Friendsville.

The only place I felt solace was inside my house. I had memories, actual memories of Graham and the things we did together inside. Of course, there were still thoughts of what might have been while I was in the house, but I could replace them with what had been. I considered leaving and moving back home with my family, but I did not want to leave this house. Graham was still inside, and I couldn't leave him behind. If I went back to my family, I was afraid that I would forget him or that everything that happened was just a dream.

The house was going to be my whole world now. The rest of it was too cruel.

Chapter Fifteen

I became obsessed with completing the renovation of this house. I thought that finishing it and turning it into a bed and breakfast was what Celia wanted me to do. I thought that bringing back to life the thing that meant the most to her would finally give her peace so she could rest.

I thought that I followed her clues. Just about everyone I told my plan to said verbatim, "this town could use a bed and breakfast." The letter that she wrote to me calling the house her whole world flashed in my mind. Showing me the love she had with Graham in the house spoke to me saying that this house needed to be loved.

The days turned into weeks because renovating a house was no easy feat even if it was just the first floor.

"Ned," I asked, nearly every day, "how much longer do you think this will take to complete?"

He had come to the point of ignoring the question, but today he wiped his brow and pulled me into a quieter area of the room to answer.

"Well, the floors are done, the bookshelves next to the fireplace still need to be built and we are waiting on the cabinets and the appliances. We still haven't started on converting the garage into your living space, so it is going to be a while."

I had wavered back and forth about whether to go with the idea of converting the detached garage into a small innkeeper cottage where I would live or not. I finally settled on doing it so that I could stick to my original idea that all the bedrooms inside the house would be for the guests. "If we leave that for last, how long do you think it will take to finish just the inside of the house?"

"Where are you going to stay in the meantime? Assuming you are going to start booking guests as soon as we are done?" Ned asked, laughing at my enthusiasm to open.

"Ned, I will sleep in my car if I have to," I said, meaning it. "But let's be real, filling up five bedrooms right away would be a good problem to have."

"Okay, you're right," he answered, finally understanding that I was being serious. "I'd give it a month." I knew that was just an estimation that he was placating me with, but it felt good to have a date to shoot for. I wanted the house to be completed as soon as possible, but I also needed to be ready when it was.

I needed to show everyone that it should be my bed and breakfast. I actuslly did Google "how to run a bed and breakfast" and found online classes to figure out how to be successful. I went to seminars and I talked to people who were in the business. I made sure that I had all the proper licenses, insurance and that everything in the house would be up to code. I came up with a solid business model. After Derek and Sam would leave my house each night, I stayed up late doing endless research. Then I started arranging partnerships. Dotty agreed to supply the coffee and pastries in exchange for advertising to my guests to eat lunch and dinner at Dotty's. I tried to think of anyone else who had a business in town that I could partner with. I realized as I tried this that there wasn't much in this town. Why would anyone come here to even need to stay at a bed and breakfast? I hated to admit it, but Derek was right, this town was dying, and it needed help. I decided to finally ask him what the plan was for the town, beyond the scaled model I had seen at his house. Soon, I told myself, soon I would ask him. I knew that when I brought up the subject, I would have to fight for my house to have a place in his plan. I would also have to show him the deed and I was not ready to do either.

Sam was still coming over every day. Ned was teaching him how to build a house and turning over the tools to give him a hands-on experience. I loved that Sam was a part of this. He was growing so much from this experience. I was proud of him. I was also terrified every time he picked up a tool, but Ned assured me that he wouldn't let him use power tools without proper training.

Derek still came over every night for dinner and to watch a movie or a TV show. Since the kitchen was unusable, Derek brought dinner with him every night, usually from Dotty's, but sometimes it was his own creation. He refused to let me pay for anything. He said that if he had to pay someone to look after Sam every day it would cost him much more than dinner. So, I let him.

We were close to being caught up on everything in the Marvel Universe. I had no idea what we would watch at that point. It was a challenge keeping space to watch TV as the renovation was coming further along. We would change the whole arrangement of the "sitting area" to accommodate for tools and flooring and walls that were in the way.

The day Sam and I took the cribs out of the nursey was a sad day for me. I couldn't tell him why and I wasn't even sure why I was sad, but he could tell I was in a funk.

"I think we should name the rooms," Sam said out of the blue, probably trying to cheer me up.

"What?" I asked, half laughing not sure if he was kidding.

"Seriously, it's a thing for B&Bs. I looked it up. If you name the rooms you can tell guests that they are staying in the so-and-so room and it sounds fancy," he explained, nudging me to play along.

I had read something about that in my research, but I brushed past it because I wasn't great at naming things. My childhood pets were "Brownie," my brown dog, "Hammy," my hamster, and "Fish," my pet fish. "Okay well, there are five bedrooms. What should we name them?"

Sam thought for a moment and said," How about naming them for the Infinity stones from the Avengers. There could be the 'Space Room,' the 'Soul Room,' the 'Time Room,' the 'Power Room' and the 'Mind Room?'"

"What about the 'Reality Room,' I asked, referring to the stone he chose to leave out.

"No one on vacation wants reality," he answered glumly.

"Okay, but I don't think those names match the feel of the old house – not that it hasn't been our underlying theme during this whole thing," I acknowledged.

"How about 'The River Room,' for the Troubled River?" Sam asked timidly this time like he was afraid of being shot down again.

"I love it. That is perfect," I squealed. I am glad that he didn't suggest "The Troubled Room" instead. I would have a hard time deciding which room that would fit – all of them maybe.

We brainstormed for a long time going back and forth on what could work. In addition to "The River Room," we settled on "The Magnolia Room," "The Rose Room," and, "The Friends Room." For the final bedroom, I knew what it would have to be called "Celia's Room" because it just was. Sam was right, naming the rooms was a great idea and managed to cheer me up.

By the time we came up with all the names, Derek was home with dinner. For tonight's feast, he brought Dotty's famous chicken pot pie and chocolate cake for dessert. If this kitchen was not completed soon, we were all going to gain a hundred pounds. It was so delicious in the meantime.

Tonight's TV watching set up had us squeezed into the farthest corner of the room away from the kitchen. We managed to get the TV and the smallest sofa in the corner, but no room for a chair.

"I have just the thing," Derek said, disappearing to his truck and coming back in with an oversized bean bag chair. "I had a feeling it was going to come to this." He laughed placing it on the floor where Sam jumped into it with a smoosh. I could just see the beans exploding out of it and sticking to the fresh paint against the wall.

Sam turned on Marvel's Agents of S.H.I.E.L.D where we left off the night before. Normally I would watch intently, but tonight I was preoccupied. Part of it was that I wanted to work up the nerve to ask Derek about the plan for the town. I didn't want him to take my curiosity as surrender. I just wanted to prove to him that my little B&B would fit in and I also wanted to know if there was ever going to be a chance to make any money. The other part was that the sofa was small, and Derek and I were sitting extremely close together. He had his arm over the back, the way he usually sat but I nearly had to sit on his lap to fit comfortably.

"I'm sorry," I said as I bumped against him for the twentieth time.

"I can't get comfortable."

"Well, if you are going keep banging into me, you might as well just get over here," he teased. But then he pulled me over to him so close that my head was resting on his chest.

He was warm, and his jersey t-shirt felt soft against my face. I could feel his chest expand as he breathed in and I could hear his steady heartbeat. He smelled like fresh linens and that hint of faded cologne. I was beginning to wonder what that cologne smelled like in the morning. I sighed, feeling comfortable and safe in his arms. Until I realized that was not the feeling I needed to have about Derek.

I started to squirm. I could feel his heartbeat quicken. Oh no, I thought, was I turning him on? Sam was sitting right next to us in the beanbag chair on the floor. I felt as awkward as a teenager with her first boyfriend trying not to let her parents catch them in the basement. It was all too much for me. I sat up abruptly and in doing so smacked him right in the nose with my head. I heard him yell out in pain.

"Oh no, I'm so sorry," I said as I moved away from him and saw that he was holding his nose in pain. "Ice, we need ice!" I got up and scurried into a kitchen with no appliances and certainly no ice. I turned back around to him. I could see that his nose was bleeding.

He stood and walked over to me. "It's okay," he reassured. *Or lied. I'm not sure.* "I just need a cold face cloth. Is there one upstairs?"

I nodded my head and led him up the stairs to the bathroom guiding him, so he could hold his head back and catch the blood in his hand. We reached the bathroom and I had him sit on the toilet, so I could find the face cloth and run it under cold water. I had to leave the room to find it. When I got back, he had toilet paper jammed in his nose and was laughing at me.

"Okay, I might be running around like a crazy person, but you are the one with toilet paper up your nose." I laughed too. I tried to calm myself to take care of the situation. I don't know why I was acting so insane. Normally I was the picture of calm in emergency situations, and I wasn't sure a bloody nose even constituted an emergency. I got the rag and ran it under the cold tap and gave it to him to put on the bridge of his nose. He held it there for a few minutes with his head tilted back and neither of us spoke.

"Let me see," I said a few minutes later, as he brought his chin down and removed the toilet paper from his nostrils. I put my hand on his cheek as I examined his nose to see if the bleeding stopped.

"I knew you always wanted to punch me in the face," he said. I expected a follow-up wink but either his face hurt too much to wink or he was not kidding.

"I have thought about it, but this was truly an accident," I told him, maybe sounding like I was kidding or maybe not. I took my hand off his cheek and started to turn to refresh his cold rag in the sink, but he grabbed my hand and pulled me back to him placing my hand on his cheek again.

"Did I trigger them?" I asked, expecting to be kissing him any second, but nothing happened.

"No," he said, looking into my eyes. I felt a pang of disappointment, but then the way he was looking at me gave me my own feelings. I wanted him to kiss me. I wanted to feel the way Celia felt when she was with Graham, but I wanted it to be just me and Derek. I held my breath in anticipation. He smiled taking my hand off his cheek and sweetly kissing the palm of my hand.

"We should get back to Sam," he said, still holding my hand, leading me back down the stairs. When we got back to our seats, he was fast asleep on the giant bean bag chair. I nudged Derek for him to look. We found a blanket and covered him.

Turning off the TV so Sam wouldn't miss any more of the show, the room got quiet. The light was low, and we were basically alone. I couldn't let this turn into a romantic moment, I thought, changing my mind about wanting that kiss. I needed to keep him talking so that nothing would happen between us. My mission was to make him fall in love with the house, not me and certainly not vice versa.

"Tell me about your plan to fix the town," I said out of the growing darkness.

"What?" he asked, sounding shocked at the question.

"All I know about your plan to revitalize Friendsville is knocking down my house and turning it into a parking lot. There has to be more to it than that," I offered, encouraging him to tell me more. "Anything else getting torn down?" I was goading him, trying to at least get him to tell me in defense of himself.

He snorted at the question. "First of all, I have been working on this for two years. This town used to be a mill town. The Mill is that old abandoned building at the edge of town. It used to be a thriving industry, but eventually, it wasn't, and the mill closed. Friendsville was lucky to survive, but all these years later it barely is."

"I can see that now that I've been here a while and trying to launch a new business," I told him, letting him know that I was with him in theory.

He perked up a little deciding that maybe he could just tell me the ideas instead of having to defend them. "Okay, then as a citizen of this town you have the right to know. Everyone else in town has some idea of the plan and is on board," he stated. "I have been working with the owner of a major hospitality company. We have a meeting with the town council and the mayor in two months. I've convinced him that we could turn this town into a vacation getaway. The town would start a tour company offering guests white water rafting packages, walking trail tours, swimming excursions in the river, hiking adventures, fishing expeditions and, even history tours. Guests would need somewhere to stay so he will purchase what is currently vacant land and build a hotel. I have put together a marketing campaign to draw people into the town. Everyone in town will be employed either by the recreation company or the hotel. Some people will convert or update their businesses to accommodate the changes. I want to bring in all of these new things without losing the small-town charm though."

I had to admit it sounded like a solid plan. Everything he was proposing would surely help the town and its residents. "So, you don't think a historic house converted into a B&B would add to the charm of the town more than say a parking lot would?"

"Holly," Derek began, but before he finished his thought, Sam started to wake up.

"It's late," I said, looking at the clock. It was only 9:06 p.m., but I wanted to stop whatever he was going to say next. "You should take him home."

Chapter Sixteen

Ned and his team finished the house a few weeks later, a few days ahead of schedule. There weren't any apocalyptic moments where the team had to stop working because of some unforeseen problem costing three-thousand dollars more like in the home improvement shows. Other than some minor repairs to the outside of the house, things went exactly as planned. I was beyond grateful. On the final day of work, the team was so close to finishing they asked if they could work longer to just get it done. I agreed, but I doubted that any of us expected it to be after midnight before they left. When I finally got to bed, all I could think about was how nice it would be to sleep in the next day – thankfully, a Saturday.

My cell phone rang early the next morning. At least it felt like it was early, checking the time I saw that it was 9:06 a.m. It wasn't that early after all, so I answered. It was my mother.

"Good morning sweetheart," she greeted. She was always chipper in the morning. As a teenager that drove me crazy.

"Good morning, Mom," I answered sounding groggy. "Guess what? The house is finished! The contractors worked late to complete it just last night."

"Oh, Holly that is wonderful news!" she said with genuine enthusiasm. "No wonder you sound so tired."

"It looks fantastic. Now I just need to book some guests and my B&B will be officially open!" I told her, skipping several steps of what I still had to do before any of that could happen.

"Well, your father and I want to be your first guests," she told me with motherly support.

"Of course, Mom, I would love it if you came to visit," I said, realizing how much I missed them. Even though I hadn't lived in their house for a long time, it was still nice when we lived close enough that I could pop over to their house for dinner or just to check in on them. My dad was close enough to help if I had any trouble with my car and sometimes, he would fix little things in the townhouse so we wouldn't have to wait for Perry's family to get a handyman. Now that I was living three hours away, a spontaneous pop in and leave was impossible.

"Great, your father and I took off on Monday, so we will be there tomorrow," my mom said, unexpectedly. "Oops, I hear someone at the door. I better go. We will see you tomorrow. I'm so excited!"

Then she hung up. I didn't have the chance to tell her that I wasn't ready, like this weekend ready, to have guests. I considered calling her back and asking to reschedule for another time, but then I remembered her saying to me that she and my dad took off work before I told her if the house was ready or not. They had planned to come and check on me regardless.

I sprang out of bed with the determination that this house would be perfect by tomorrow. I jumped in the shower and threw on some clothes. I went downstairs to start with some coffee from my brand-new dream kitchen. By the time I reached the bottom of that stairs and looked around, my dream turned into a bit of a nightmare. Typically, Ned and the crew would clean up after themselves, but at the late hour when they left, they didn't have the time or energy. He offered to come back today to clean, but I told him that I had plenty of time to do it myself.

I pulled my phone out from my pocket and dialed.

"Hello," Derek answered, knowing it was me. Ever since the night I accidentally gave him a bloody nose, our conversations had been strained. Not because he was mad that I clocked him in the face, but because of our unfinished conversation about the town and my place in it. It was like something was hanging over us that we needed to talk about to clear the air, but neither of us wanted to initiate the conversation. I put that aside now because I needed help.

"Hey, can I borrow Sam today?" I asked hopefully.

"I will ask him. What's up?" he questioned. Maybe he heard some panic in my voice?

"My parents are coming," I started to explain.

"Hey Sam," I heard him yell after covering the phone. "Will you go to Holly's today to help her with the house?" I could hear Sam's muffled answer in the background. "Sure," Derek said, talking to me again. "We will be there in thirty minutes."

"Thank you!" I said and hung up the phone.

I looked around. There was so much to do that I wasn't sure where to start. On top of the construction dust and occasional nail, there were boxes and boxes of things I ordered for the house. Thankfully, earlier in the week Sam and I took a little road trip to drop off the bags of sellable things to the consignment shop I found online, and then to the dump for anything we considered to be trash.

In one of the many boxes, I unearthed the cleaning supplies. By the time Sam and Derek arrived, I had the kitchen sparkling clean. That was not too hard to accomplish since the appliances were all brand new, including my spectacular dishwasher. I was admiring it when they walked in.

"Wow," said Sam, "everything turned out great! Are they finished?"

"Yes, they stayed late last night because they were almost done and didn't want to wait until Monday. I think Ned has another job coming up that he wanted to start," I informed him.

"Yeah, it looks really good or it will by the time we're finished with it," Derek said, looking around like he was trying to figure out where to start. I hadn't expected Derek to help – just to drop off Sam and do something else with his day. Why would he want to help do anything in a house that he was just going to have demolished? But that did work nicely in my plan to make Derek love the house. If he worked on it with me, he would feel some ownership of it. That could certainly work to my advantage.

"Okay great, you're staying. Another set of hands is welcome. Thank you," I said and tried to figure out how to break up the tasks for each of us to get things done as efficiently as possible.

Since I already finished cleaning the kitchen, we moved on to the dining room and sitting room. Those rooms were not too bad either. It was a matter of picking up drop cloths and pulling off the tape. The house looked shiny and new. Even upstairs where the contractors hadn't touched looked amazing. Sam and I took down all the wallpaper and painted each of the five bedrooms. The carpet in all but Celia's room was in near perfect condition – just needing to be cleaned. Celia's room was almost the only room in the whole house that seemed lived in.

"Okay, guys. You're probably going to think that I am a total nerd, but I drew out each room and everything that goes in it," I confessed.

"You are a nerd," Derek teased and took the papers out of my hands. "But wow, these are great. Is any of this finished?"

"Nope," I answered. "That's why you two are here." I smiled at their weary faces.

"Well, let's do it then," Sam suggested. "Where do we start?"

The truth was that a lot of it was already finished – the most difficult part. Somehow, I was able to charm Tucker and Slim into bringing furniture down from the attic which was terrifying to watch as they maneuvered down the tiny pull-down staircase. They managed to do it though. The bed, the one that was to be Celia and Graham's marriage bed went into the "Friends Room," which was the former nursery. There was a dresser in the attic that I had them put in that room as well. I found an antique bedroom set at the consignment shop where I took the things I wanted to sell from the house. Basically, I traded all that stuff for the bedroom set and paid to have it delivered. That set went into the "River Room," which was formally the child's bedroom because there needed to be more than a twin bed in that room if guests were going to stay there. Luckily, the room was big enough to fit the new set including the twin bed, and the twin matched enough with the new set that it didn't look out of place. Maybe a family traveling with children would stay in there, I thought. The "Rose Room," the guest room I had been using as my bedroom already had a queen-size bed, as did the "Magnolia Room," the first bedroom Sam and I cleaned out and then of course "Celia's Room" did as well.

With most of the bedroom furniture in place, we just needed to set up the rooms. Sam and I already organized sheet sets with the accompanying duvets, so the beds just needed to be made up. I also had boxes prefilled with other décor items assigned to each room. I was so proud of my organization when we were each able to take a bedroom and knew where everything was supposed to go. Even with that, it still took most of the day to complete. When we finished, Sam and Derek ran to Dotty's for carryout dinner. There was no way I was cooking today. While they were gone, I took the time to admire each room.

The "Rose Room" might have been my favorite although I was partial to it since that was where I was living since I came to town. The carpet was already pink so Sam and I painted the walls a cream color because painting them pink would have just been too much. The duvet I picked out was covered in giant pink roses in tribute to Celia's previous giant floral theme that ran throughout the house. I found a local artist to paint canvases of roses that matched the duvet and hung four of them on the walls. The dresser with an attached mirror was covered with bright white doilies which were originally there. I found a YouTube video showing how to get them from their dingy state back to bright white. On top, I placed an oversize pink vase with extra-large artificial red roses that stood out but didn't clash with all the pink in the room.

The "River Room" with its dark blue carpet and two different-sized beds proved a bit of a challenge. I found the perfect matching duvets in queen size and a twin that had a design like the bends in a river with complimenting shades of blue and beige running through them. Sam and I painted the walls of this room a light shade of blue so that all the blue wouldn't be overwhelming. I found a local photographer who had photographs of the Troubled River in the same spot during all four seasons. I pictured the beauty of the river in autumn the first time I came to town and I was right, but it was beautiful in all seasons.

The "Friends Room," is named such because of the two cribs. I imagined that if there had been two babies sharing that room, they would have grown up as the best of friends. That room had dark blue carpet also, but unlike the "River Room" we painted the walls white and I found a duvet that was red with a stitched design. That was the room that had the privilege of housing the original bed and a passionate bold red bedspread felt right for it. McFarland's Market, of all places, was where I found the wall hanging for that room. Greg McFarland, the grandson of the original owner had vintage signs that were once used in the market just collecting dust in the back office. I saw them one day when I held the door for Greg who had his hands full. He was so happy that I was interested in them, he just gave them to me.

The "Magnolia Room," was another room with dark blue carpet and we painted those walls cream. I found posters of large magnolia flowers online that were almost the same as the wallpaper in Celia's bedroom. I thought that magnolias must have been her favorite flower, so I wanted to honor that. I left a bit of the history that Sam and I unearthed in that bedroom by putting the rotary phone on a side table and made a large binder and put the old newspapers we found safely in plastic sleeves for guests to flip through if they were interested.

Finally, there was "Celia's Room." It was so difficult to redo that room, but I thought that Celia would be happy with a fresh start. Since the carpet was so worn, I had it torn up and the hardwood floors underneath restored. I decided to decorate that room with vibrant colors to match Celia's personality when she was young. A striped duvet on the bed and a red area rug underneath. For the walls, I had prints made of old family photos. I wondered if they would be too personal to hang on the walls for guests to look at, but I realized that to them they would just be old photos of people they didn't know.

By the time I finished admiring our work, Sam and Derek came back with dinner. I went downstairs to eat for the first time in my brand-new kitchen. I could smell whatever amazing feast Dotty's had provided for us and my stomach growled in anticipation.

"I can hardly believe how different this place looks," Derek said in between bites of fried chicken. "You have an eye for design."

"Thanks. I once worked for an interior designer," I revealed.

"What job haven't you done?" he asked, which put me on the defense immediately because people always criticized me for that but then he continued. "I think if your aunt had a different path in life, she would have tried on a lot of jobs to see what fit first too. You both have moxie." I decided to take his comments as a compliment since his tone seemed genuine.

"Are we finished working?' Sam asked hopefully with his mouth full of chicken and was about to dive into the coleslaw. I smiled and waved my arm out in front of me to show that massive room on the other side of the kitchen that was completely empty. He sighed and took a drink to wash down his dinner.

I laughed at his pain. "There isn't that much left to do down here. I special ordered a dining table from Charlie who makes furniture on the side. He promised to bring that tomorrow. For now, I just need two rugs unfurled in the dining room and the sitting area and there are a ton of books that need to come downstairs and go in that bookshelf." I told them. My volunteers both groaned at the idea of carrying books.

"What else is going down here?" Derek asked, looking at the space.

"I need some furniture for the sitting area and something for the walls, but I know my mother will want to help so I'm going to let her go shopping with me."

Nodding with understanding and possibly relief that there was no additional furniture to move, Derek scooped Sam up with his arm around his shoulders and headed upstairs to get the books. The boxes were too heavy to carry down the stairs, so we made a human chain to get them all down. Derek was upstairs, I was downstairs, and Sam was in the middle. It turned out to be a good idea and we were done in no time.

Sam came downstairs and asked to watch the TV that was above the fireplace, while I arranged the books on the shelves down both sides. I agreed and let him know that I was paying for my own WiFi and no longer "borrowing" it from the church.

I had the shelves almost done and Sam was almost that the end of the TV show he was watching when I noticed that Derek hadn't come down the stairs yet. I went up to make sure he was all right. I found him sitting on Celia's bed holding a familiar green book in his hand. I meant to put that journal back in the trunk in the attic with the others, but I forgot. He was focused on what he was reading when I came into the room and he didn't seem to notice me. His face was pale, and I thought I saw tears in his eye. I realized he was reading about his own grandfather's death. I left the room without saying anything. I would just let him catch up with Celia's story on his own.

Chapter Seventeen

*T*he dining table arrived the next day before my parents. It was so
massive that Charlie had to bring it through the front door in pieces
and then assemble it in the dining room where it would reside. It was
stunning. I wished that I could have afforded to use cherry wood like the
rest of the furniture in the house, but a table big enough to seat twelve
people would have cost a fortune, and quite honestly, I was starting to
run out of money as it was. No matter, Charlie had crafted and stained
the wood to nearly match the other furniture and gave it a polished look
by finishing it with a gloss. Charlie also made twelve chairs stained to
match the table, they were simple high back chairs constructed of five
wooden slats with straight legs and upholstered seats, with red material
reminiscent of the look of chairs popular in the 1940s. Once the table
was together and the chairs arranged, this room was starting to look
ready for guests. I hoped I was as ready.

"Charlie," I gushed, "this is the perfect table. It is exactly what I wanted. Thank you so much."

He smiled, "Thank you for asking me to build it. Contracting is my job, but furniture making, now that's my passion."

"I can tell," I said, running my hand over one of the seat cushions.

Charlie fidgeted for a moment with one of the chairs, like he was inspecting it for quality, but then spoke. "Holly, I was wondering if you might like to go out to dinner with me sometime."

"Oh," I said, completely taken off guard. Charlie seemed to be a great guy. He was attractive, creative, smart and had a career and at least one hobby that I knew of too. But in all the time we spent together working on the house, I hadn't really thought of him that way. In fact, the time that I thought he accidentally triggered Celia and Graham and might kiss me in the kitchen, I was thinking of ways that I might have been able to stop him.

"It's okay," he said as though he had heard my answer without me speaking it. "Ned told me that you were with Derek Sterling, but I thought I would take a shot anyway."

Ignoring his original question, I said, "People think that Derek and I are a thing?" I knew that in this town, if Ned thought that Derek and I were a couple, everyone did.

"Well, I guess. I mean, are you?" he asked, sounding hopeful that maybe we, in fact, were not.

I wasn't sure how to answer. I wanted to say that we were absolutely not a couple and something dramatic like he was my arch nemesis like in all the superhero movies we were watching, but I wasn't sure that was true anymore. We spent every weeknight having dinner together with Sam and curling up in front of the TV. Sometimes even on the weekends we went to the river or had a picnic. He just spent his entire Saturday helping me get the house ready for my parents' visit when he could have literally done anything else. We never went out without Sam, so it wasn't like we were dating. All of it was part of my plan to make him feel at home in the house so he wouldn't want to tear it down, right? We established this set up as a way for me to take care of Sam during the day. It was no more than a civil agreement, I tried to convince myself.

Charlie spoke, breaking me away from my thoughts and realizing I hadn't answered either of his questions. "I can tell that whatever you have going on with Derek is complicated, so I am not going to try to complicate it more. I'll see you around. If you need more furniture for the place. Let me know," he said sincerely then turned and walked to the door.

I felt bad about leaving things like that, so I started to follow him. Before I could say anything, he opened the front door to find Derek standing outside holding a bouquet of red roses. Charlie snorted or maybe snickered and greeted Derek with a pat on the shoulder and walked to his car, shaking his head.

"Hey," Derek said to me as he stepped in the house. "Was I interrupting something?"

"Uh, no. Charlie was just setting up the table," I said, admiring the flowers.

"I thought you might need something for the table. The artificial flowers in the rooms are nice, but fresh flowers might be a nice touch for your parents' visit," he offered. He seemed embarrassed. Maybe it was unexpectedly meeting Charlie at the door or maybe he was rethinking the meaning of the flowers he chose.

"They're beautiful," I said, taking them from him. He smiled with relief. "Come in and check out the table and chairs." He did and was admiring the craftsmanship as I went into the kitchen to retrieve a vase and water. I set the flowers on the counter while I searched for the table runner I set aside to use on the dining table when it arrived. Finding it, I carried it and the vase of roses to the table to set it up. "Perfect. Thank you, Derek."

Derek brushed it off as though it was no big deal and asked, "What time are your parents arriving?"

I looked at the clock. It was 9:06 a.m. "They should be here by ten. I am going to take them to Dotty's for breakfast." Derek raised an eyebrow and I said, reading his mind, "Yes I know this is supposed to be a bed and breakfast, but I wasn't sure that the table would be set up by the time they arrived. I will let them have the bed first and serve them the breakfast tomorrow."

Derek laughed. "Well, I will get out of your hair then."

"Actually Derek, would you and Sam like to have dinner with us?" I asked. That felt like it came out of nowhere to me, but I wanted my parents to meet them.

Derek flushed a little. "Sure, Sam will love that."

At 10:00 a.m. on the dot, my parents pulled into the driveway. Seeing them get out of the car, I realized that I really missed them. I couldn't wait for them to see the house. My mom stayed back and looked up at the house like she was trying to conjure whatever memories she had of being here before. From the sound of it, there were not many pleasant ones. My dad, on the other hand, bounded up the steps and met me on the porch with a bear hug. He let me go and took notice of the enormous porch. Sam and I painted the three rocking chairs white and I finally got the red geraniums that I dreamed of put in hanging pots.

"Holly, this house is incredible," my dad said with true admiration.

"You haven't seen anything yet," I told him with promise as I reached around him to hug my mom.

"Oh, Holly this house looks warmer and friendlier than it ever did before," she said her, voice cracking like she was trying to hold back tears. I wasn't sure if they were tears of pride or relief that this was no longer the house in her memory. I hoped it was a bit of both.

I opened the front door and ushered them both inside. My mother audibly gasped. Once again, I hoped that it was a good thing. I gave them a short tour and explained the changes I made. My mother remembered what the kitchen looked like before the renovation and was astonished. As we went around the house, she kept pointing out things that used to be in certain places. I guess it was like a memory game she was playing, but it was starting to upset me.

"Mom, do you not like that I made changes to the house?" I asked, trying not to sound as annoyed as I felt.

"No, the house looks amazing. It's just so full of memories for me. I'm sorry. I didn't mean to make you feel bad for changing things. I think you did a wonderful job," she assured me, giving me a tight hug.

I felt a sense of relief. I didn't realize how much I valued my mother's opinion on this. Deep down I worried that changing the house, wasn't the right thing to do, like I was ruining family history. My mom's approval felt like she was speaking for everyone in the family who knew this house and it felt good that she approved.

"We are so proud of you Holly," my dad added and that was all it took to bring me to tears. I had searched so long for my purpose and I finally found it. I was glad that my parents knew that and didn't think it was just another thing I wasn't going to commit to. This time it really was different.

As my mom and I wiped our tears, I noted that the bedrooms needed tissue boxes. I laughed at myself and showed my parents to "The Rose Room" where they would stay the night. I moved out of that room and into "Celia's Room" the night before. I wasn't ready for anyone else to occupy that room just yet.

"Have you guys had breakfast yet? I want to show you one of my favorite places in town," I told them. They hadn't eaten breakfast and readily agreed to go.

We walked the short distance to Dotty's Diner from the house, past the church where I found Sam that day under the stairs. I told my mother all about Sam including how I first met him on many phone calls we had together, so I made sure to point out that landmark. We arrived at Dotty's and my dad opened the door for us, the bell alerting Dotty that she had customers. As usual she was at the front with a coffee pot in hand. I introduced her to my parents, and she told us to grab a seat and she would of course bring us some coffee. We chose a booth in the back. My parents sat together on one side facing me as I sat on the other.

"So how are you doing?" my dad asked.

"I'm great," I said, fully meaning it. "I am so excited about the bed and breakfast. I just need to start marketing it and book some guests."

"That's terrific," he gleaned. "You know this would be a great weekend getaway spot for my co-workers. It's far enough away to feel like a vacation, but it doesn't take that long to get here either. If you have business cards, I would gladly pass them out at work." I felt a little embarrassed for him to do that. It reminded me of the time when I was in middle school and we sold gourmet chocolates and gift baskets for the school band fundraiser and my dad took the order form to work and asked his co-workers to buy them. It worked though. I was in the top sellers' club. Maybe it wouldn't be such a bad idea. I would take all the free advertising I was offered.

"Thanks Dad. I'll make sure to give you some before you leave. I'll take all the help I can get."

"Now that you have all that worked out. I want to hear more about this Derek," Mom interjected.

"They are really cute together," I heard Dotty chime in as she flipped my mother's cup over and filled it with coffee.

"Dotty," I said sternly, "we aren't cute together. We aren't together at all. We are barely even friends. I'm just caring for his nephew during the day."

"The lady doth protest too much, methinks," my dad said, quoting Shakespeare.

Dotty smiled and nodded in agreement with him. I just shook my head. Clearly there was no changing anyone's mind about Derek and me. Luckily, everyone stopped talking about it and we ordered our breakfast. What we did talk about was the town and my dad's job – he sold insurance, and my mom's new yoga class she had just started. It was so good to have them here.

Dotty placed the bill on the table, and I reached for it, refusing to let them pay. Breakfast at Dotty's was cheap, so I was not exactly breaking the bank. "Humph," I uttered after looking at the total.

"Is it too much? I can take care of it," my dad offered.

"No, it's not that at all. It's just the total is nine-oh-six, and I keep seeing that number everywhere I go," I explained.

"Seeing repeating numbers means something," my mom declared. "Hold on, I have an app." She reached in her purse to pull out her phone and glasses. Slowly touching the screen to type in her password, she entered each number with purpose while looking over her glasses. Yoga was only one of the many holistic approaches she took on life. She was big into healing crystals for a while and meditated daily. I was not surprised she had an app for this. I guess even the people searching for a centered life relied on smartphones.

"Okay, here it is. The angel number 906 is reminding you to pay attention to important things in life and to focus on making your life more meaningful," she read directly from the app.

"I thought I was focusing on the important things in life. I found my purpose with this bed and breakfast. That's meaningful, right?" I asked.

"Holly, I know you don't believe in these things, but your angel is trying to tell you something," my mom said. *Oh Mom, if you only knew.*

"When did you start seeing the number? Before or after you started working on the house?" my dad asked. He didn't believe in half the stuff my mom did, but he always supported her crazy notions. Although this time it might not be so crazy. I mean no crazier than my dead aunt possessing my body and making out with her old boyfriend who was possessing the body of his grandson. I thought for a split second that I might tell my mother about it. If anyone would believe me it would be her, but then I thought better of it.

"While I was working on the house and since, I think."

"Well maybe you aren't focusing on what you should be. Like somewhere you missed the point," my dad offered his interpretation.

"Then what is the point?" I asked frustrated, thinking that Celia was trying to tell me I was doing the wrong thing with her house.

"Maybe love," my mom offered. "Maybe you are supposed to stop focusing so much on your career and should be focusing on finding love instead."

For a moment I thought Aunt Celia had possessed her too. I read all her journals. I felt how much she loved Graham. I knew that love was all she ever wanted, and that house became her prison as she tried to bask in her memories of love instead of finding it again. I had to just sit for a moment to process how I had missed something so obvious.

"Or it is a complete coincidence and a load of crap," my dad said, breaking me out of my thoughts. He must have seen the pensive look on my face and was worried that they upset me. I smiled at his efforts.

After I paid the check, we walked back to the house. I asked my mom to help me figure out the final touches for the house via online shopping and my dad took a book outside to read on the bench next to the fishpond. It was a lovely and relaxing day.

My dad offered to cook dinner for us, disregarding my protest, mostly because he wanted to try out my new kitchen. He was the one who I got my love for cooking from. I offered to go to the market to pick up what he needed, but he declined that as well saying he wanted to pick out the ingredients himself. I conceded and then had to tell him that we would be having two more for dinner – Sam and Derek. I could feel my mother smiling behind my back.

Dad returned from the market about thirty minutes later and he was not alone. "Look who I found on my way home," he announced as Sam and Derek followed him inside.

He found them? How did he even know who he was looking for?

"We caught Ben at the market. He was asking people if they knew his daughter, Holly who was opening the B&B on Maple Street," Derek explained, winking at me. "We were there because Sam wanted to bring you something."

Ben, he called my dad Ben, now? I rolled my eyes like a thirteen-year-old girl. Sam then distracted me with chocolate cake. "I was going to try to bake a cake, but I think you might need to teach me how," Sam confessed with a smile.

I smiled back. I adored that kid. He changed so much since the first day we met. He was always a sweet boy, but now he seemed like a happy one too. He and Derek were getting along so much better. I was a little sad that he would start school soon. I was going to miss not having him spend his days with me anymore. With the house finished, I wasn't sure what we were going to do now anyway. Apparently baking lessons were his plan.

"This is my favorite cake ever," I told him, getting another smile. "I will most certainly teach you how to bake."

I returned my focus back to Dad and Derek, the newest best buddies. "Derek, this is my wife Caroline," my dad said introducing them. Instead of shaking his hand or giving a tiny wave like a normal person, she decided to reach out and hug him. He smiled and took the hug graciously, like he was hugging his own mother. Then Derek went into the kitchen to help my dad with dinner. *What was happening?*

To make things worse, I couldn't stop thinking about my angel number interpretation and how Celia was trying to tell me to find love with Derek. Having that in the back of my mind was making me awkward toward him. I couldn't help blushing every time he looked in my direction. I was clumsy and flaky and ridiculous.

Clearly, he noticed because he followed me into the kitchen as I was getting the cake. "Is everything okay with you tonight?" he asked.

"I'm fine," I said quickly because I was lying. I needed to get out of kitchen and not be alone with him. I grabbed the cake and some plates to take back to the table. I actually wished I could invoke Celia's spirit in that moment so my awkwardness would go away. That would probably be a bad idea with Derek so close to me. It occurred to me then that Celia and Graham hadn't been around since the changes were made to the house. I wondered if we wouldn't be able to trigger her and Graham again. Not that I really wanted to, especially not now with my parents here.

I pushed my intrusive thoughts out of the way and sidestepped Derek to take the cake to the table. "Who wants cake?" I asked, setting the cake and plates down. A unanimous, "I do," came from my parents and Sam so I began cutting into the cake placing each slice on a plate to which Sam added a fork and passed around the table. As I cut the final slice for myself there was a knock at the door, I laid down the cake knife and wiped my hands on a napkin before walking over to the door to answer it.

"Hello," said the mail carrier as I opened the door. I hadn't received any mail at the house yet, so I didn't know her name. I would have to learn it for the future. "I'm sorry to bring this so late, but I have a certified letter that requires a signature." I signed for the letter and thanked her, forgetting to ask for her name. I was distracted by the seeming importance of the letter.

My guests were too absorbed in their own conversations to pay attention to me. Seeing that it was a mail carrier at the door must have satisfied their curiosity enough to ignore what I was doing. I opened the letter immediately and my heart sank in my chest. It was typed on the official letterhead of attorney, Anthony Cohen. It was a cease and desist letter representing their client, Derek Sterling, demanding I stop any changes to the house and business ventures thereby. I felt nauseous. I felt angry. I felt betrayed.

I interrupted Derek's conversation with my father by slamming the letter down on the table in front of him. Suddenly all my awkward giddiness regarding him had left me and was replaced with rage.

"Derek, what the hell? You had this sent to me now? After I sank most of my money into this place? How could you?" I tried not to cry, but the tears came anyway.

"Holly," he started, sounding confused. He looked at the letter, and realizing what it was, his face soured.

"Don't. Just don't," I croaked out through my tears. I could barely look at him.

He stood and put his hands on my shoulders to try to get me to face him. I shrugged him off. "Please, you have to let me explain," he begged.

"Was all of this just a game to you?" I yelled, channeling my tears into rage instead. "Did you think if you pretended we were one big happy family that you could just charm the house out from under me? Or maybe you were just going to sue me and take everything anyway." I glared at him, daring him to speak so I could shut him down again.

"It wasn't like that!" he said, raising his voice indignantly. He took a breath and calmed his tone. "Come into the kitchen and talk to me. Let me tell you my side," he pleaded.

Before I could say anything else to Derek, Sam started to cry.

"Sam, I'm sorry. I don't think it's a good idea if you come over tomorrow," I told him as he was sobbing. That was the part that nearly broke me. *See I would make a terrible mother anyway.*

Sam's face was so confused. I couldn't bear to look at him and I didn't want to hear anything from Derek. "You need to leave," I snapped at Derek.

As I walked upstairs to my bedroom I saw my parents' faces – wide eyes and mouths agape. *A disappointment to them once again.*

From upstairs I heard the clanking of dishes, muffled conversation and finally the front door open and close again. I knew it was only a matter of time before my parents came upstairs to find out what was wrong. So, I waited.

After ten minutes or so, when no one came upstairs, I went downstairs to look for them. They were both in my kitchen. My mother was rinsing dishes and arranging them in the dishwasher while my father located plastic containers and was packing the leftovers from dinner into them. When I got to the kitchen, they both saw me at the same time and stopped what they were doing.

"Hey," I said, sheepishly.

"Holly," my dad started cautiously, "I think you may have overreacted." Was he serious? Was he going to take Derek's side over mine?

"Dad, did you read the letter?" I asked. I honestly was not sure because he had always backed me up on everything.

"I did," he confirmed. Now I was getting upset again, but I refused to cry like a little girl to her daddy.

"You didn't give Derek a chance to explain himself," my mother chimed it. I shot her a wounded look, but she continued anyway. "He said that he had his attorney write that months ago before you started working on the house. He thought you had already received it and just chose to ignore it."

"Why would I ignore a letter from an attorney?" I asked, trying to discredit that statement and expose it as just an excuse.

"Well, it is a cease and desist letter – not an order from the court," my dad explained. "Derek said he thought you probably received it, and someone named Randy probably advised you to ignore it."

"Randy - Mr. Sullivan," I said, bringing the formality back into our relationship. "He was Celia's lawyer and now mine I guess."

"With a cease and desist letter, the sender can choose to take further action or not," my dad informed.

"The bottom line is that Derek said he isn't going to sue you," my mom confirmed.

I walked back into the dining room and flopped carelessly on one of my new chairs. My parents followed me in and pulled up to the table.

"I really made a mess of this," I said, wallowing in my own self-pity.

"Yeah you did," my dad blatantly agreed. My mother shot him a dirty look. "What? She did."

"Thanks Dad," I said sarcastically.

"What happened to the Holly who opened the door to her beautiful new home to us this morning? That Holly was an adult. That Holly had her shit together." Another look from my mom stopped him from continuing.

Wow. Tough love much? He was right though. I was becoming a different person since I moved here and took on this house. I was making my own way and doing a great job if I did say so myself. Now was not the time to revert to my old ways.

"It's okay Mom," I said so she would stop with her death stare on my dad. "Dad, you're right. I completely overreacted."

My dad looked at me proudly like he knew I had it in me.

"Oh God, Sam! I was so callous to him," I said, putting my head down on the table.

"Kids are resilient, Holly. He will be okay. Just make sure you go over there and fix things with him," my mom offered kindly.

"I will," I promised, lifting my head. "What if Derek does sue me now?"

"He's not going to sue you," my mom assured.

"How can you be so sure?" I asked.

"Because he's in love with you, dummy," my dad answered, grabbed my mother's hand, kissed the top of my head and they both walked up to their room before I had a chance to protest that idea.

Even though my dad thought he and Derek were suddenly best buds, knowing him for a few hours didn't make him an authority on how Derek felt about me. He's my dad of course *he* thinks everyone loves me. I wasn't so sure. I also wasn't so sure Derek wouldn't take the house away from me.

My biggest problem now was that Derek had every right to sue me. The deed I found in Celia's jewelry box proved that the house was only in Graham Sterling's name and Celia had no legal right to it and therefore, neither did I. How could I be so naïve? I was so busy being brave and coming up with my big plan to make Derek fall so in love with the house that he would change his mind about it. I never considered that the plan could fail. What do I do now?

Chapter Eighteen

*A*fter the awful scene at dinner last night, the least I could do was bring my A-game to breakfast. I dazzled them with my extensive menu. I started with coffee, made in my kitchen, not at Dotty's for a change. I served them fresh strawberries, pineapple, and melon to start. The next course was French toast with cinnamon sugar, then eggs, bacon or sausage, and home fries with a choice of orange or apple juice on the side.

Still savoring the last few bites of his meal, my dad paused and said, "Wow kiddo, that breakfast was amazing."

I finally felt like I was doing things right. Looking for feedback, I asked, "Do you think I need to offer more choices?"

This time my mom answered, "No, I don't think so. Remember this will be a sit-down breakfast, not a continental breakfast with a bunch of choices like at a hotel."

"That's true, but I could change the breakfast menu each day of the week so my guests don't get bored, and if they don't like something they can try something else the next day. Maybe I could come up with a different breakfast every day for a month," I added.

"I like that," my dad concurred. "You could also do pastries."

"And pancakes. Oh, or blueberry bread and homemade waffles," my mom suggested. *Note to self: Buy a waffle iron and then learn how to use it.*

"How about crepes?" my dad said excitedly, and my mom's eyes lit up with delight. *Crepes? Cripes! I think crepes are beyond my cooking capabilities. I learned to cook at the Italian bistro down the street from us, not Paris, France, guys.*

I wrote everything down that they suggested so I could produce a formal menu plan when I was ready. I could learn how to make fancy dishes with the help of some cookbooks and YouTube videos maybe. The bottom line was my parents were raving about my food and I was so relieved.

When they packed to go home, I was sad to see them go. As my dad took their things to the car, I found my mom still in their room making sure she remembered everything. I walked into the room and closed the door behind me.

"Mom," I said sheepishly, "can I talk to you about something?"

"Of course, always," she said, sitting on the bed and patting the spot next to her indicating for me to sit down. "What's on your mind?"

I sighed deeply as I took the spot beside her, not sure if I was going to be able to tell her what I wanted to say. "I … um," I stammered, "Well, since I moved in here I have felt a strong connection to Aunt Celia."

My mom shrugged. "That's not surprising. You are now immersed in all her belongings. Sometimes you can get to know a person better through their things than what they say."

"Uh, that's not exactly it. I mean I have found out so much about her, especially from her diaries," I started. My mom cringed a little at the idea of me reading her diaries. "I know that sounds awful, but I needed to find out more about her because I think her spirit is still in the house."

To most people, that idea would sound completely off the wall, but things like this were right up my mom's alley. If there was anyone I could share this with it was her. "Oh," she said excitedly. "Why didn't you tell me about this yesterday? I would have tried to feel her spirit too."

I pictured her burning incense and chanting, and I almost laughed out loud. Realizing what I was about to tell her did not give me the right to judge, I stifled that laugh. "When I say her spirit is in the house, I mean her spirit sometimes possesses me, and the spirit of her former lover, Graham, who happens to be Derek's grandfather possesses him … and they try to … reenact their love affair through us."

Shit. Did I really just tell her that?

"Oh," she said, rubbing her hands up and down her arms like she had gotten a sudden chill. "You know when I came here as a little girl I always felt … unrest, I guess is the best way to describe it, in this house. I was timid about coming back here this weekend, but as soon as I stepped through the doorway there was a feeling of peace here instead."

I wasn't sure how to respond. She looked me in the eye and continued, "I believe you, Holly. It seems pretty obvious that you and Derek are the perfect vessels because of your own attraction to each other."

"Even if that were true. I ruined everything with Derek last night," I lamented.

"I don't think that's true. You just need to talk to him," she told me, cupping my chin in her hand.

"There's more," I said dryly. She looked at me like she couldn't imagine anything more. I took another deep breath. "I found the deed to the house in one of Celia's jewelry boxes. Her name isn't on it. The house was owned by Graham Sterling only."

"Oh no. So that means the house wasn't hers to leave to you," my mom said, telling me what I already knew. "Derek was okay with you renovating the house anyway?"

"Well, I kind of haven't told him," I confessed. It was not my proudest moment.

"Oh Holly," she started, sounding disappointed, but then quickly switched her tone to hopeful. "Tell him. Things will work out the way they are meant to and if the way he looks at you has any bearing on his decision, he's going to let you keep it."

"Everything okay in there?" my dad bellowed before I was able to respond. Then he opened the door and charged through.

"Yep, all good," I answered, standing and not looking at my mom.

"Just having some girl talk," my mom said, standing up next then asking my dad, "Car all packed?"

"Ready to go," he answered as he turned to walk downstairs, realizing that he had interrupted something.

My mom took my hand and walked with me downstairs. She stopped just as we got to the porch and turned to me saying, "Be brave, my girl."

I smiled and walked her the rest of the way to the car where we hugged our goodbyes and I told them that I hoped they could try to come for a visit every few months. I knew that once I started this business, I would have little time to visit with them.

My dad came in for a second hug and said, "We are so proud of you." It was exactly what I needed to hear.

I waved at their car as it pulled out of the drive and until it was out of sight. I knew my mom would probably fill my dad in on the deed to the haunted house thing on the way home. They always told each other everything. I was pretty sure that was the secret to having a great relationship.

I knew exactly what I needed to do next.

Chapter Nineteen

I pulled out my cell and dialed Derek's number. He picked up on the first ring. "Hi. It's me," I said, not sure what to say next.

"I was worried that you were still mad at me. Are you still mad at me?" he asked. I could hear him brace himself for the answer.

"No, I'm not mad at you. I'm the one who acted like a lunatic last night. I am so sorry," I said softly. "Is Sam okay?"

He blew out a sigh before he spoke which I knew wasn't good. "He's been in his room reading comics for most of the day. I think he's okay though."

Derek definitely did not believe that. I could tell that my behavior last night had a damaging effect on Sam. I would have to think of a way to make it up to him. That would have a wait a bit though because I needed to spill my secret to Derek first. I would have to do it in person. *Be brave.*

"Do you think you could come over tonight?" I asked hesitantly, almost like I hoped he would be too busy.

"Sure," he answered happily. "Do you want me to bring dinner?"

"That's okay. I'll cook," I offered. It was truly the least I could do. We made plans for him to come over at 6:30. I sighed and walked into the kitchen to see if I had enough groceries to put something together or if I needed to stop at the market. It hit me like a ton of bricks that this could very well be the last meal I cooked in my beautiful new kitchen. Derek would have every right to kick me out and knock down the house. I fingered the papers with the breakfast menu notes that my parents and I had just dreamed up, and thought about how that might be all it ever was – a dream.

I left the kitchen to go upstairs and decided to go up to the attic. There wasn't much left up there. I scattered the furniture throughout the house along with any knick-knacks that seemed to go with the décor. A box of Celia's things that I brought up from her room was sitting on the floor next to the chest full of her journals. Looking at the chest gave me a sense of hope. I still hadn't felt her presence since Derek and I invoked them at the river. That seemed like such a long time ago. I missed her.

Opening the trunk, I took all the journals out and laid them on the floor. I carefully pulled out the wedding dress and placed it on the remaining table set against the wall. I hadn't thought to see if anything else was in the trunk before. Looking in I pulled out a tarnished jewelry box and a police dress uniform that was obviously Graham's. She put it in with her most cherished things because above all else she cherished her time with him the most. I thought I would offer it to Derek. Maybe he or even his father might like to have it, although explaining where he got it to his father might be a little tricky for Derek. *Perhaps it was time for Thomas to know the truth.*

I picked up the jewelry box and opened it to find it lined in blue velvet with its precious contents cushioned inside. Tucked in the velvet were three rings – a man's wedding ring, a woman's wedding ring, and a simple engagement ring with a setting that held one beautiful diamond. I opened the box of Celia's things from her room and found the watch that had been on her dresser. It seemed like it belonged with the rings in the jewelry box, not just tossed aside in a cardboard box with her other less meaningful trinkets. Even when I packed the watch, I didn't look at it closely. I hadn't been ready to see what I knew was on the back from my vision in Celia's room. Holding the watch in my hand, I turned it over before placing it into the jewelry box. It was engraved with the words "To the man I love, on our wedding day. Always and Forever," just like it had been in my mind's eye.

The feeling of the tragic loss set in again and I began to weep. The emotion was so strong I couldn't stop it. I knew I was crying Celia's tears. I wailed and let everything out that Celia had bottled up for all those years.

As I regained control of my senses, I found I was still clutching the watch in my hand. I wiped my eyes as I sat up a let out a deep breath. A sense of relief, Celia's relief, washed over me and I hoped maybe now she could move on.

Finally setting the watch into the jewelry box, I put the box and the wedding dress back in the chest. I left the uniform out to offer to Derek and put all but the 1946 journals back in the chest. Later I wanted to read all the entries from that year just to feel Celia's love for Graham one more time.

I climbed down from the attic and decided I needed to have lunch at Dotty's. It was about 2 p.m. by the time I walked to the diner. Being well past the lunch rush and ahead of the dinner rush, I entered the diner to find I was the only customer. Yet for some reason, Dotty was still there at the front to greet me with her coffee pot.

"Do you ever sit down?" I asked her, laughing.

"Nope. You sit too long, and you die," she answered. "You want to pick a booth?"

"Okay if I just sit at the counter today?" I asked.

"Of course, okay if I straighten up some things while you do?" she asked.

"Oh yeah," I answered. "Do you need any help?" Dotty smiled and shook her head. "No, I mean do you have any jobs you might need filling?"

Dotty stopped what she was doing to look at me with surprise. "Why would you need a job? Things not going well at your B&B?"

"I haven't opened yet and even if I do things are going to be slow at first. I'm going to have to support myself somehow," I told her even though this truth was a revelation to me at the moment as well.

"What do you mean *if* you do?" she asked. That was a question I didn't want to answer right now. Luckily, she took my silence as a lack of confidence and decided to give me a pep talk. "When my husband and I opened this place forty-something years ago we were terrified. We sunk everything we had into it and lived on love for the first few years. He was the one who insisted we call it Dotty's. The thing is that this was our dream and you have got to make sacrifices to make your dreams come true. If you work hard enough and provide a good service, the customers will come. Don't worry honey, if you need a job until that happens, I could always use a waitress."

I smiled as she asked for my lunch order. When I requested a salad and water, she asked if I was on a hunger strike. She was not one to mince words.

"Dotty, did your husband pass away?" I asked, preparing for my condolences.

"Nope, he left me for a younger woman and moved to Vegas. I loved the old fart though," she confessed. "I probably still do." With that, she disappeared into the kitchen and returned with my salad, water, and a cookie on the house.

"Let's not talk about me. Let's talk about you and Derek," she prodded and raised her hand to stop me as I opened my mouth to reply. "And don't tell me there is nothing there, my coffee pot is really a crystal ball and I can see all."

I smiled at her persistence. "Oh Dotty. It's so complicated with Derek. We are definitely not more than friends, if we are even friends at all I'm afraid."

"That's funny because my crystal ball here," she started, holding up her coffee pot, "sees a family when it comes to you, Derek and Sam."

"We do spend a lot of time together, but that's because I take care of Sam while Derek is at work," I explained. I certainly didn't want to tell her I was trying to make Derek feel that way so he wouldn't tear down my house.

"It also sees how that man looks at you when you aren't paying attention – like you are the most precious thing to him. He does nice things for you. How many times has he picked up dinner here so you wouldn't have to cook? I was watching the first time he laid eyes on you, I mean after he stopped yelling at Randy and noticed you sitting there. He was stunned silent. That's a thing I've never seen before," she concluded.

I started to say something to reject her notions and to tell her about the time he parked two bulldozers in my front yard and threatened my house, but ever since that kiss on the stairs – the one that Celia and Graham shared – things had started to change between us.

"Besides seeing him as gorgeous and successful, because that goes without saying, how do you feel about him?" she asked, then backpedaled with, "If you don't mind me asking."

How do I feel about him?

Mom said seeing the number 906 means I need to focus on love but am I in love with Derek or is it just Celia's feelings for Graham projected onto him? No. I have my own moments with Derek, like on the couch that night when I curled up against him.

He's sweet.

He's a good dad to Sam.

He's kind and generous.

And … I think I am falling in love with him.

I mean, he helped me fix up my house. The house he said wasn't mine which truly isn't mine. Which I have to still tell him about. Which will make him hate me again.

We will be back to where we started – at war. So, I can't fall in love with him. I can't have feelings for him. I can't see us as a family.

"Nothing," I lie out loud, protecting my heart. "I'm sorry Dotty, but your crystal ball is broken. I've got to go. Thank you for lunch." I grab my purse and start for the door. When I take a glance over my shoulder Dotty just lifts her coffee pot at me and gives me a smirk.

Truth bomb. I finally figure out that I am in love with Derek and in three hours he is going to hate me for keeping the deed a secret. Why did it always take me so long to figure out the right things for my life? As I walked back to my house, I considered just not telling him. I could burn the deed, and no one would ever be the wiser. It was the only proof in existence that the house was only in Graham's name. That just didn't feel right. What would Celia do? I knew the answer to that. She would be brave and tell him the truth. So that is what I was going to do.

Chapter Twenty

For the first time since we met, I was nervous about Derek coming over for dinner. Not in the same silly schoolgirl way I felt the night we had dinner with my parents, this time was different. I had so much to lose following the truths that I would reveal tonight – my house, my purpose, the man I … love.

What do you wear to have dinner with the man you once despised and had kissed several times while not actually in your own body, but recently realized you had your own romantic feelings for while lying to him for most of the time you knew each other and were planning to serve a confession with dessert? A mini dress. You wore the shortest, sexist damn mini dress you owned with the hope, if nothing else, of distracting him.

After establishing the dinner menu – Eggplant Florentine with fire-roasted tomato sauce and toasted ciabatta bread, for which I stopped for ingredients at the market and the produce stand on my way home from the diner – I ransacked my closet to find the perfect dress. I decided on a dark green one patterned with small white flowers, white buttons down the front, and capped sleeves. The dress came to about six inches above my knee which would make bending over a challenge. Pairing the dress with my high strappy black sandals made it appear shorter. Instead of feeling insecure, as I had the other times I had worn this dress, tonight I felt confident.

With dinner in the oven, I came down to the kitchen to toss a salad. Partly because it would be a good pairing with the eggplant dish and partly to give me something to do while I waited for Derek to arrive. I also had wine chilling in the refrigerator that I would serve before and during dinner. I realized that subconsciously I had cultivated all the components of a date – special dinner, a nice dress, wine – all I needed now were some candles and soft music. Considering it for a minute, I decided to forgo the candles and music deciding that might be too over the top especially since I hadn't actually told Derek that this was to be a date.

Promptly at 6:30 p.m., the doorbell rang, and I tried to calm myself before answering it. I took a deep breath and smiled as I opened the door to find Derek and Sam. I'm not sure why I was surprised that Sam came along. Wasn't that our thing – the three of us? Why wouldn't Derek bring Sam? I hadn't told him otherwise. Suddenly I felt over-dressed and foolish.

"Wow," Derek said. "You look incredible." He had trouble taking his eyes off me which was the idea, so maybe not a wasted outfit after all.

"Thank you," I started hesitantly, "But I really need to apologize to both of you for the way I acted last night."

"That's okay Holly, we make mistakes sometimes. Can we come

in? I'm starving." Sam asked. Just like a kid to forgive and forget so easily.

Luckily, I hadn't set the table yet or there would have only been two plates instead of three and I wouldn't have wanted Sam to feel like a third wheel or Derek to feel bad for bringing him. Also, there was plenty of food to go around. I asked Sam to help set the table and whisked him out of the kitchen every time I had to bend over to check the oven.

With salad, bread, and dinner finally on the table we all sat down to eat.

"Your parents are great," Derek said, trying to make conversation.

"Yeah, your mom was asking me if I was ready for school and told me that I would make lots of friends," Sam added.

"Thanks," I smiled. "They really liked the both of you too."

Then there was an awkward silence.

What had I expected though? Last night had ended so badly and even though I apologized I wasn't sure if that was enough to make it right. Maybe it was just because I was acting weirdly nervous and putting out a pseudo-date vibe that made things feel out of balance.

Derek tried to address what he thought was the elephant in the room. "Holly, I just want to apologize again about last night. That letter couldn't have shown up at a worse time. I asked my lawyer to write it months ago before I really knew you. I guess he finally got around to it and sent it out without alerting me."

"It was brought to my attention that I may have overreacted somewhat, and it was wrong of me not to let you explain," I said, glad that we were talking again. "I'm sorry too."

"I just want you to know that I would never sue you over this property. This house is yours," Derek continued.

That would have been the perfect opening for my confession about the deed and the house not actually being mine, but I didn't take it. I couldn't force the words out. Derek had fallen for my plan to make him so comfortable in the house that it felt like home, but unfortunately, I felt the same way and I couldn't bear the thought of ruining it. So instead I just gave a big smile and continued eating my dinner.

When we were all finished eating and cleaning up, Derek announced, "I have a surprise!" He walked out to his truck and returned with the DVD of the latest Marvel movie which was also the last one we needed to watch to finish our marathon. Sam jumped up and down with excitement and Derek smiled at me hoping I would share Sam's joy.

"That's perfect. I can't wait to watch it," I said, hopefully with believable enthusiasm. I looked at the uncomfortable sofa that was still one of the only choices of seating besides Sam's bean bag chair near the TV above the fireplace. "I think I'm going to change though."

I came back downstairs a few minutes later, but instead of my sexy dress and sandals, I was wearing a tank top, sweatpants, and flip-flops with my hair piled on top of my head in a messy bun. I didn't wash my makeup off, so I still had that going for me. Comfort was the basis of our relationship and who was I to change that? While I was upstairs, I located the deed to the house, folded it, and put it in my pocket. At some point tonight, I was going to have to work up the nerve to show it to Derek.

"Are we ready now?" Sam asked impatiently.

"One more thing," I said retreating to the kitchen. I could hear Sam groan, but I thought he would be okay with waiting when I brought out dessert – brownie sundaes with hot fudge, whipped cream, and a cherry on top. I brought the first one out and handed it to Sam. The way he grabbed it from me, I was sure he had forgiven me for prolonging the movie. I hurried back into the kitchen to make two more sundaes.

"Do you want to just share one?" Derek called from the other room. I obliged by only making one more sundae and brought out two spoons. As I sat down on the sofa, I realized that I could have split it into two bowls so we could each have our own. Derek didn't seem to mind and took a spoon from me as I sat down. I never thought about how intimate sharing a dessert could be but sitting closer to him by the necessity for both of us to reach the bowl and spoon wrestling for a bit of brownie with the most fudge felt a bit like foreplay.

Conscious that sharing ice cream could have been something that Celia and Graham had done, I handed the rest of the bowl to Derek not wanting to risk conjuring them in front of Sam. Or maybe I was just afraid of my own feelings. Either way, Derek happily finished off the rest and we eased back into the sofa to watch the movie.

"You look beautiful no matter what you wear, even sweats," Derek whispered to me. Sam was so engrossed in the movie, I doubted he would have noticed even if Derek shouted it. I smiled and blushed and then pretended to be focused on the movie too. What I was focused on was the fact that Derek had inched closer to me and the arm he usually rested on the back of the seat was brushing my shoulder. I decided to go with it and snuggled into him resting my head on his chest. He pulled me closer to him with the arm that was on the back of the seat. We just sat there in that position for most of the movie.

When the movie was over, I looked down at Sam excited to hear his reaction and talk about what happened like we always did. Sam, however, was fast asleep. I wondered how much of the movie he missed. I poked Derek in the side to get his attention and then pointed to sleeping Sam. It seemed early for Sam to be asleep, so I checked the time on my phone. It was 9:06 p.m. because of course, it was.

"Why don't you just carry him up to one of the rooms and he can spend the night?" I suggested to Derek, hoping it didn't seem like an invitation that was extended to him as well.

"You don't mind?" he asked, sincerely worried about inconveniencing me.

"No, it's fine. Can you carry him?" I asked, thinking that if he couldn't, he might as well just wake him up and take him home. But Derek scooped Sam up in one swoop and started up the stairs. "Any room except mine is okay." I whisper shouted at him.

I knew that there was a good chance of something happening between us when Derek came back downstairs. It would be the first time in a long time that the two of us were alone together. I couldn't let that happen with my lie still hanging in the air. I got up from the sofa and stood at the bottom of the stairs. I needed to tell him as soon as he came down. No more excuses.

It seemed to take Derek forever to come back down. "I put him in the River room, I think. He woke up a little bit and I told him that you were letting him spend the night and then he immediately fell back to sleep." Derek explained, smiling.

I felt the ice cream curdling in my stomach with every step closer Derek came. I knew I had to just tell him and get it over with. "There is something I need to show you," I blurted out before he even got to the last step. I reached into my pocket, pulled out the deed, and gave it to him, bracing myself for his reaction. His face blanched and I knew that whatever was coming next was not good.

"Where did you find this?"

"It was in the bottom of one of Celia's jewelry boxes," I answered, not offering anything additional.

Then he asked the question I dreaded. "When did you find this?"

I promised myself that I wouldn't lie to him about it anymore. "A month or two ago." I blurted out again and then drew in my breath and held it.

"A month or two ago you barely had anything rebuilt in the house." He started working out the timing in his head and then sounded angrier with each word. "You could have stopped fixing up the house and showed this to me."

"Yes, you're right. Construction had just started, but I was already invested in the house. I thought that if you could just see how amazing this house was going to be that you wouldn't want to tear it down and then the name on the deed wouldn't matter," I explained, thinking now my reasoning sounded flimsy at best.

"You didn't give me a choice," he said, running his fingers through his hair. He was pacing the room now as he spoke. I stood in the same spot at the bottom of the stairs, leaning up against the wall.

"I was going to tell you, but I found it the day that we all went to the river together for the first time. It was such a great day that I didn't want to spoil it. Then there never seemed to be a good time after that. I thought with the three of us spending so much time here that you might start to think of this as home and us as ..." I trailed off, not brave enough to finish my sentence. That is when the uncontrollable tears started, and I couldn't speak.

"So, this was just a plan to save the house?" he asked, sounding hurt. "You never cared for Sam and me at all. You were just manipulating us?"

"No!" I objected. "It wasn't like that. We just fell into a natural rhythm. Getting you to change your mind about the house would just have been a bonus." Okay, maybe part of that was a lie. I did originally plan to make Derek feel at home, but the truth of the matter was that it was so easy to do.

He stopped pacing the room and walked toward me getting so close that he pressed me up against the wall, his face just inches from mine. "Do you want to know what is true?" he said, his face so close now I could feel his breath on my skin. "I never asked for any of this. I was just a single guy doing whatever I wanted and then my brother died and suddenly I was a single father and then we met you and we were acting like the perfect little family. And you know what?" He paused, a single tear running down his cheek. I was afraid that whatever he said next would tear me apart and I was right. "I loved every single minute of it and now I know it was all just a big lie."

He pushed away from me and started to walk toward the door still holding the deed. I wanted him to stop so I could tell him that it wasn't a lie and that I loved every minute of it too, but I knew there was nothing I could say that would stop him from leaving. Except for one sentence. "Graham, please don't leave."

He turned around, facing me, and managed to say, "You summoned them?" before a force pulled us together and he swept me up in his arms and kissed me. I knew it was unfair to summon the spirits of Celia and Graham with the last words she ever spoke to him. But I needed Derek to come back. I needed to feel the way Celia felt about Graham just one more time. The kiss was so powerful maybe because Celia knew that this would be the last kiss or maybe because my emotions mixed with hers and made it that much more intense.

Then just as in the past, it felt like a switch turned off and we were in control of ourselves again. Derek looked into my eyes before he let me go. I saw hurt and sadness in his eyes. He released me from the embrace and without saying a word, he left just as Graham had that final day. I feared that like Celia I had just lost my love forever.

Chapter Twenty-One

Sam woke the next day full of energy and enthusiasm. He bounded down the stairs like he just had the best sleep of his life. If every guest who slept at my B&B woke that way, I would surely have a thriving business. When Sam found me in the kitchen trying my hand at making scones, it was clear he had slept through everything that happened with Derek and me last night.

"Good morning," I said, trying my best to sound cheerful though I was certainly not feeling that way. "Want to try one of my scones? They will be ready in a of couple minutes."

"Okay, but I'm a little bummed," he said. *Oh no, had he heard the argument after all?*

"Oh yeah, how come?" I asked worried about what he heard.

"Because I slept through the movie I have been waiting to watch forever!" he explained.

Relieved, I told him that Derek had left the DVD and he could watch it after breakfast. Joy returned to his face. I didn't want to dim his joy again, but I thought I should tell him some version of what happened last night, so he wouldn't be surprised when the three of us no longer spent time together. My heart sank when the reality hit me that Derek might not allow Sam to spend time with me anymore.

"There's something I want to tell you," I started, feeling almost as nervous as I had telling Derek the truth.

"Okay, what is it?" he asked, snatching a hot scone right off the baking sheet and putting it on his plate.

"Derek is angry with me and for good reason. I lied to him about something," I told him, trying to weigh my words. He stopped trying to eat the scone that was too hot anyway and looked up at me. "I kept a secret from him about something important and it was just the same as lying."

"What was it?" he asked like he was tired of the build-up and just wanted me to get to the point.

"Remember the deed to the house, the important paper, that said who the house belonged to that I was looking for?" I asked. He nodded encouraging me to continue. I took a deep breath. "Well, I found it a while ago and it says that your great-grandfather was the real owner of this house and not my aunt. She was kind of stealing it by living here and didn't have any right to give it to me."

Sam thought about it for a minute and then went back to trying the scone. "My mom always told me that if I did something wrong, I should tell her because if she found out about it, it would be a worse punishment because lying is worse than telling an ugly truth."

"That's right," I confirmed. "The thing is that since the house is not mine, Derek can ask me to leave and tear it down. If that happens, I don't want you to be mad at him. I brought this on myself. If I just told him when I found the paper it might be different."

Sam considered this for a moment. "Holly, there's something I've been lying about too." I couldn't imagine what he was going to say. What could he possibly have to lie about? "I think that Uncle Derek was always going to tear the house down and I should have told you that, but it was so much fun fixing it up together."

"Why would you think that?" I asked, wondering if Derek had said something to him about it.

"I saw a model of the new town on his desk and the spot where the house should be, was just a flat parking lot," he confessed, hanging his head a little and looking at the plate while he talked.

This was something I already knew, having seen the model accidentally that day I was looking for the bathroom in Derek's house. "I know about that buddy. I saw it at your house that day when your grandfather was visiting. I saw it by accident," I told him trying to take away his guilt.

"Oh, except last week Uncle Derek was working with the people who make the model to update it for his town council presentation, but the spot where the house should go is still a parking lot."

For a ten-year-old boy, he was way more insightful than I gave him credit for. If Derek had changed his mind, and like he promised, was not going to turn the house into a parking lot, wouldn't he have had some scaled model of the house put into the empty spot? Was Derek's anger at me last night an easy way to blame me when the house came down anyway? Was my lie assuaging his guilt?

There was a knock at the door that startled both Sam and me. Getting up from my stool at the breakfast bar, I walked to the door to answer it. Derek was standing there when I opened it which was strange because normally he would just let himself in.

"Hi," he said flatly. "I'm here to pick up Sam." He could barely look at me. Before my conversation with Sam, I would have thought it was because he was still angry with me, but maybe it was his shame that was the cause.

I nodded. "Sam, Derek is here," I announced.

Sam came to the door and Derek greeted him with a smile. "Hey bud, did you get a good night's sleep?"

"Are you going to make Holly leave?" Sam asked, looking Derek directly in the eye. Oh, kids, I forgot about their honesty and lack of filter. I felt flush with embarrassment. Now Derek would probably think I was filling Sam's head with things to get him on my side – if I even had a side that is.

Derek was taken aback by the question and looked up at me with shock on his face. I wasn't sure if I should say something to explain, but before I could, Derek collected himself and answered. "Not today."

Sam seemed satisfied by that answer and went over to the DVD player and retrieved the disk of the Marvel movie, placing it carefully back into its case. "Okay if I take this home to watch it?" I wasn't sure if he was talking to me or Derek, but we both said, "Sure," at the same time. Sam ran over to me and hugged me tightly at my waist just in case he was never going to see me again I guessed. When he released me, Derek ushered him out the door gently with an arm around his shoulders and turned slightly to give me a weak wave and the two walked out and got into Derek's truck and drove away. I went out to the porch to watch until they were out of sight. I was heartbroken.

I went back to the kitchen to remove the last batch of scones from the oven. They were dried out and hard, nearly burned but not quite, from being left in the oven a little too long. I slammed the baking sheet on the stovetop and started to cry. What was I going to do?

I always felt comforted, somehow, by reading Celia's journals. So, I went upstairs to retrieve her 1946 journals I had stored under the bed in her room. I took them to my bedroom and plopped on my bed to read. I already knew the beginning and the end of her story, but I wondered if there was something in the middle that I missed.

July 13, 1946

It was hot today, but it was a special day because Paul and Thomas's maternal grandparents were taking care of them for the day. It happened to be Graham's day off from work as well. That meant we got to spend the whole day together.

Most of the time we only had a few hours to spend together each day and we chose to spend that time in the house. Because we were not ready to tell people about our relationship, we never ventured out together. Today was going to be different. Graham told me to pack a picnic basket because we were going to a hidden spot he found by the river. He told me he came across it while he was on patrol one day.

I was so excited to be out with him. I packed the picnic basket with sandwiches and fruit and a red and white checkered tablecloth to make it seem fancy. This is probably a terrible confession, but I secretly hoped that someone would see us together, and then we would have no choice but to tell people about us.

The spot he found was just under the bridge and he had to park his car on the side of the road, and we walked down a hill to the edge of the river. There was not a soul in sight. We spread out the tablecloth on the ground and sat on the grassy knoll at the river's edge and ate our lunch. The river was so relaxing to watch. It looked cool and inviting and I was disappointed that we did not bring swimsuits. I teased that we should just strip down our clothes and skinny dip in the river. I was only partially joking, but he got serious and told me that he had arrested people for doing that.

I just laughed it off, but then I sensed his apprehension about being there. When I asked him about it, he said that I was just being silly that he was having a perfectly lovely time. When we heard a noise he nearly jumped out of his skin. It turned out to be a bird swooping the water to catch a drink. I told him that I surely was not being silly. That turned into our first fight. We might have been louder about it except we were afraid that someone might hear us. I accused him of being ashamed of me and started to walk tearfully back to the car.

He took my arm and pulled me against a tree to give me a quick peck on the lips. He said he was going to prove that he was proud that I was his girl and he was going to carve our initials in the very tree that we were leaning against and he did. He took out his pocketknife and carved GS + CA and scraped a heart around it. He told me that those initials would remain there for a hundred years which was not even close to how long he would love me.

I was happy then. We walked back to the car hand in hand and returned to our house where we made love for hours.

I stopped reading and thought about the entry. When Derek and I saw the initials in the tree, we had a completely different experience than the one Celia described. They hadn't even gone swimming that day much less brought a raft to flip over and make out under. I skimmed through the rest of the summer entries of that year and I couldn't find a single entry where they had kissed in the river. Maybe she was projecting things on us that she wished happened. It didn't sound like that was their best day together. Maybe she wanted to rewrite history. I didn't know how any of this spiritual divining worked.

I still hadn't had enough of her journals and wanted to keep reading a little while longer. I was up to September now and stopped to read the entry on the day of the 6th – 906.

September 6, 1946

Today was the happiest day of my life. Today Graham and I got married!

We took a bus to the city and got married at the courthouse. Graham surprised me the day before with news of this plan. He said that he could not bear one more day that we were not husband and wife. He wanted to make an honest woman of me he said. I was delighted and happily agreed.

We decided that we would wait to tell our friends and family. We would invite them to what they would think was a New Year's Eve party and surprise them with another wedding ceremony so they could all be a part of it. I thought that plan sounded so romantic.

Graham had another surprise for me. It was wedding rings! He told me he was so sorry that he never gave me a proper engagement ring. After buying the house, money was a little tight, but he had a wedding band for me and an engagement ring with a huge beautiful diamond in the center, and of course a wedding ring for himself as well. I would have to remember to get him a token for our wedding ceremony in December that he could cherish as I did this diamond.

I wore a simple white dress and Graham wore his dress uniform and we promised to love, honor and obey until death did we part in front of a judge and two witnesses that the court provided. It was not the wedding of my dreams, but I married the man of my dreams, so it did not matter.

I am too excited to share anymore today. I promise a longer entry tomorrow dear diary. Goodnight from Mrs. Graham Sterling.

I closed the journal in utter shock. My hand gently brushed over something that fell out from the journal as I placed it on the floor. Opening the neatly folded paper, I discovered it was Celia and Graham's marriage certificate that must have been tucked into the crease of the diary all these years. I needed a few minutes to collect my thoughts. Celia and Graham got married? I sat with that for a few more minutes.

The number 906 that I was continuously seeing was pointing me to this journal entry. I should have known that Celia wouldn't hide a message in a questionably interpreted numerology concept. That was not her style. She always spoke her mind and got right to the point.

She wanted me to read this entry. But why? So that I would know that she wasn't a spinster like the whole town thought or a slut like the other diary entries made her out to be to someone like me who was reading the story and not living it?

Then I had an epiphany. If she was Graham's wife at the time of his death, wouldn't that mean she inherited his estate unless there was a will that stated otherwise? Meaning - this house would legally be hers. Thereby giving her every legal right to pass down the house to the heir of her choosing, namely, me? What if Graham didn't have a will? What then? I had the marriage certificate as proof. It was time to call Mr. Randall Sullivan, Esq. immediately.

Chapter Twenty-Two

When I picked up the phone to call Randy, I saw that I had a voicemail from Derek. I played it immediately.

"Holly, I'm calling to see if Sam is with you." His voice was shaky. I couldn't tell if it was because of worry or because he was talking to me. "Please call me."

I pressed the call back button and started down the stairs to look around the house. I doubted that Sam would be there, but he knew he could let himself in, so it was worth a look. Derek answered before the phone had a chance to ring.

"Is he there?" he asked, skipping the pleasantries.

"No, I don't think so. I was upstairs for a long time and I'm looking around the house now to see if he just came in. I don't see him. What happened?" I asked, trying to remain calm. Sam had a history of running away and it was by luck that I found him the last time.

"He's mad at me," Derek said, not needing any further explanation.

"Pick me up. I'll help you look," I demanded and hung up. I thought if we found him together, he might be more willing to come home.

I took a few minutes to look around the yard. Sometimes Sam would take a comic book out by the fishpond and sit on the bench to read. I wished him to be there today, but he wasn't.

Derek and I hadn't even considered Sam's feelings. If Derek and I admitted that the three of us felt like a family, surely Sam felt that as well. He had just lost his parents months ago and here we were, his new "family" in turmoil. No wonder he ran away. He probably thought that he didn't belong anywhere. His relationship with Derek was improving, but it still wasn't solid. In my plan to make Derek feel at home in the house, I never thought about how Sam might feel the same way. I told myself that I was just his babysitter, but that wasn't true. I felt so much more for him than that and likely he felt the same about me.

I met Derek in the driveway, so I could just hop in his truck without him having to waste any time coming into the house to find me. I was near tears by the time he arrived.

"Where do we start looking?" he asked, broken, and probably feeling as guilty about this as I was.

I instructed him to pull into the church parking lot. I doubted that Sam would hide in the same place twice unless he wanted to be found, but it was worth a try. I got out almost before Derek stopped the truck and ran over to the stairs in front of the church. Nothing.

I took a minute to look around the parking lot at other potential hiding spots like behind the donation box and the shed in the back. No Sam.

At this point, Derek parked the truck and we walked down the street to Dotty's diner, hoping that he was just hungry and wanted a place to lay low for a while. We were greeted by Dotty in her usual upbeat fashion, but her face dropped when we told her why we were there. She hadn't seen him, but she promised to keep an eye out and call us if she did.

Stepping outside the diner, we both looked up and down the street trying to think of a place Sam might go. The lack of anything interesting enough in the town to draw in a ten-year-old boy emboldened the truth that the town was on the verge of death. With that glum realization, we walked back to the church parking lot and got back in the truck.

Derek started driving toward the bridge and it took me a minute to figure out he was going to the edge of the river. That idea chilled me. There were too many places for a little boy to get into trouble there. The river was calm at the end we swam in, but upstream was rapid and could easily pull you under, not to mention what the rocks along the way could do. Then there were the woods on either side of the river that a person who didn't know his way back could get lost in as well. I worked myself up into such a tizzy by the time we reached the bridge that I was figuring out how best to group a search party with all the townspeople I knew.

Derek's phone rang just he parked the truck along the side of the road. The phone was paired with the truck's Bluetooth, so it came through the speaker at high volume for both of us to hear.

"Derek?" I heard Thomas's voice bellow through the cab of the truck.

"Dad," Derek answered, trying to calm the rising panic in his voice that he undoubtedly was feeling as well. This was the last person he wanted to tell that Sam was missing. "Hey, I'm in the middle of something right now. Okay if I call you back later?"

"If that thing you are in the middle of is looking for Sam, he is here with us," Thomas said. Was that disdain in his voice? Disappointment maybe?

The feeling of relief rushed over me and I knew that Derek was feeling it too. "Thank God. How did he get all the way to your house?" Derek asked, thinking Sam couldn't have walked the whole way.

"He called me from outside the diner and I picked him up. He was upset with you, but he wouldn't tell me what was going on. I haven't pushed it yet," he warned.

"Dad, I'll tell you the story on the way there. I have Holly with me. She was helping me look for Sam. Let me drop her home and then I'll be on my way."

"Bring her," Thomas said cheerfully. "I know your mother is dying to meet her."

Derek cringed and clearly regretted mentioning me, reminding his father that he was on speakerphone and that I could hear the whole conversation. Or maybe the cringe was the idea of me meeting his mother. Either way, his response was, "I don't think that is such a good idea. I will be there soon." He pressed the button on the side of his steering wheel to end the call.

We drove back to my house in silence.

"I'm glad that Sam is okay," I said when we pulled up to the house and Derek stopped the truck. I opened the door and hurried to the house. I reached the porch and found Derek chasing after me.

"Holly, wait," he said, slightly out of breath. I must have been walking faster than I realized. I stopped just before the front door and turned around. He met me on the porch.

I was glad he followed me, and I wanted to be the one to speak first. "Last night, did I ever say I was sorry? Because I am so very, sorry."

He stepped in closer to me. "I have so many feelings that I haven't had time to sort out yet."

"I know," I assured him. I wanted to say more, but I knew I needed to give him space to think. I also didn't think this was the appropriate time to mention that Celia and Graham were already married before Graham died. I needed to find out if that meant anything legally regarding ownership of the house first anyway. In reality, I was a hopeless romantic who wished that he would do the right thing on his own and let me keep the house as a gesture of true love and I wouldn't have to mention it. Except, of course, to just tell him in general because he was the one person in the whole world who would have the same reaction I did when I read the journal.

Derek stood there silently studying my face. I almost wondered if he could read my thoughts. "There is one thing I need to do though," he finally said.

"What's that?" I asked, truly not sure what it could be.

"I need to know what it feels like to kiss you – just you and me," he said before pulling me closer and brushing his lips against mine. He started slowly, allowing me to protest if I wanted. I didn't. His lips were warm against mine and I laced my arms around his neck. He responded by deepening the kiss – his tongue gently parting my lips in search of mine. Then he stopped for a moment and looked into my eyes before kissing me again. That was not an option we had with Celia and Graham in control. When it was over. It was over. But this time when he pulled away briefly, he chose to continue kissing me. The burning passion and hunger that Celia projected through me for Graham were gone, replaced by my own desire for Derek. I wished we could have stayed on the porch together forever, but the kiss ended. And I had to let him go.

He brushed his hand all the way down my cheek as he released me from the kiss and silently turned, got back in his truck, and drove away. I hoped that he thought of that kiss the entire way to his parents' house to retrieve Sam and then the two of them would come back and we could act as a family again. The romantic in me wished again for more, hoping that maybe we would someday be a real family.

That didn't happen. I would be lying if I said I didn't wait all night for them to come back to the house. I calculated how much time it would take Derek to get there and back. When that time passed, I reconfigured the estimate to include the time it would take to explain what happened. When it was later than that assumption allowed, I thought about the time it might take for Sam to be coaxed to go home, that maybe they all talked together, that maybe his mother invited them to stay for dinner. It was 11:00 p.m. before I gave up hope and went to bed.

Chapter Twenty-Three

The timing worked out that Sam started school shortly after Derek and my falling out had occurred, so he didn't need to come to my house all day anymore. At his age, he was able to let himself into their house by himself and stay alone until Derek came home from work. I wondered why Sam hadn't stopped by to see me though. It occurred to me he ran away because of me and that maybe he thought that I was to blame for breaking us up. If that were the case, he wasn't wrong. It broke my heart to think that he was mad at me too.

To make things worse, without a decision from Derek regarding the house, my B&B venture was put on hold. I couldn't very well start marketing to potential guests to stay at the house when technically I was squatting in it myself, much like I imagined Celia thought she was doing for the last seventy years of her life. Not to mention the fact that the town still didn't curate tourism. It was a dying bed and breakfast in a dying town.

I couldn't live off what was leftover from Celia's money after the renovation any longer. So, I took Dotty up on her offer to be a waitress at the diner. The pay was not much, but she fed me for free. I was also able to learn some techniques from her for baking and pastry-making that I could use if ever my B&B opened. Derek came in only once when I was working, and Dotty graciously took his order. I hadn't seen him since then. I worried that either he and Sam were starving, or Derek was cooking every night which meant they were not eating until late. It was no longer my business though.

One morning two men wearing business suits came to the diner for breakfast. The townspeople typically didn't wear suits except to funerals, weddings, and maybe to church on holidays. Except for Derek and the mayor whose roles in town government warranted it. It was obvious that these two men, one who looked like he was in his early fifties, wearing a perfectly tailored navy blue suit with a red tie and the other, probably in his mid-sixties also wearing an expensive gray suit with a muted purple tie, were not from around here.

It was my day to hold the coffee pot at the front door and greet the guests. While Dotty got a kick out of doing this, I was not nearly as comfortable with it.

"Good morning gentlemen," I said with my usual greeting. "Please, sit wherever you like."

They thanked me and took a table in the middle. I gave them a few minutes to get comfortable before I ran them down with my coffee pot. That is how I felt every time I immediately walked over to a table and poured the coffee. It was kind of Dotty's rule to greet customers with coffee, although after all these years, Dotty had developed ease in doing that. I hadn't yet.

As I tried sauntering over and flipping their coffee cups in the hope of not disturbing them, I heard the man in the blue suit say, "So Bill, what do you think of the town?"

"I think this could become a fantastic tourist town. The potential for recreational activities has unlimited possibilities," the man named Bill replied. The other man looked pleased.

My attempt at being the invisible coffee deliverer was failing miserably. I bumped the table and nearly dropped one of the mugs on the floor. I could have been embarrassed, but my years in customer service jobs taught me to smile and just own it.

"I'm sorry gentlemen. I have not mastered the art of the delicate coffee pour," I explained, playing the new girl card. As if on cue, one of the mugs started to topple off the table, but the man named Bill caught it before it hit the floor. "That was a great catch. Thank you for the save!"

"Well," Bill started, "at least you haven't spilled any coffee."

I flashed a smile and said with a laugh, "Oh boy, you probably should have waited for me to start pouring before you said that."

The man in the blue suit exaggeratedly pushed his chair away from the table as I began pouring the coffee in his cup. He laughed when I said, "Okay, all clear."

"Well, now that I have completely interrupted your conversation, I am going to leave you alone to look at the menu and I will be back in a few minutes to take your order." They smiled brightly as I walked away, and I was positive I had won them over, which is important for a server to do as it potentially increased the tip they would leave.

I walked back up to the counter and Dotty grabbed my arm and pulled me into the kitchen. "That dark-haired man in the blue suit is Anthony Della." When I stared at her blankly, she filled in more details. "He is the hospitality bigwig who is interested in investing in the town and building one of his hotel chains here."

"Why are they here today? The meeting isn't until the end of the week," I whispered. "And who is the other guy?" Dotty shrugged at the last part.

"There's a town hall meeting tonight, so the residents can talk about their feelings on the future of the town. The town council has to make sure everyone in town is aware of what is going on and gets the chance to speak before the council with any questions or concerns," she explained. "Why don't you know this? It's been posted on the bulletin board for two weeks." She pointed over to the corkboard near the door that was covered with flyers and business cards that while put up, were never taken down. There was so much noise on that thing I couldn't bear to look at it.

"Oh, I missed it," I told her. "Can anyone come?"

"Yes, of course. I guess Mr. Della is planning on sitting in on the meeting. I'm not sure who the other guy is, maybe his partner," she answered. The white-haired man named Bill would remain a mystery for now I guessed. "Maybe I should wait on them."

Slightly insulted that she implied I might mess something up, I replied, "No, it's okay. I've got this."

With confidence, I walked back over to the table. Luckily, they were the only customers in the diner at the time, so they would have my full attention. "Have you decided on breakfast?" I asked.

"What's good here?" Bill asked, after clearly not looking at the menu at all.

"The strawberry pancakes are the best you will find anywhere," I offered, flashing another smile.

"Sounds good to me," Bill answered.

"With the works of course?" I asked, flirting a little. You know the old saying, "You get more flies with honey than you do vinegar," well I was putting that technique into practice.

"Absolutely," Bill agreed, smiling back at me.

"And for you, sir?" I asked the man in the blue suit who I now knew to be Mr. Della.

"I think I will have scrambled eggs with a side of bacon," he answered. I nodded in recognition. "Oh, and can I have a refill on the coffee when you get a chance, please?"

"You like to live dangerously I see," I said referring to my less than stellar coffee pouring skills.

I walked back to the counter and gave Dotty the order, retrieving the coffee pot and taking it back to the table. This time they both sat perfectly still as I poured.

"Holly," Mr. Della called, squinting to see my name on my badge. "You live here, tell me about the town."

I laughed to myself that he thought I was a townie, but at the same time, I liked the idea that I was. I must have shaken off my city girl roots at some point and looked like I belonged here. The truth was I had started to feel like I did.

"Well, I'm not really from here. I've only lived here a short time," I explained.

"Now I definitely would like to know what you think about the town. It seemed to me that everyone who lived here had been here forever," he explained, seeming bewildered that I would choose to live here when I wasn't just born here.

"My aunt lived here for seventy-years and she recently passed away, leaving her house to me," I told him. "What is it that you would like to know about the town?"

"First, I am sorry to hear about your aunt. I, well perhaps, we," – Mr. Della moved his hand from himself to Bill – , "have an interest in investing in this town and we would like to know if you think that would be a good idea."

It seemed like a lot to ask one person to speak for an entire town. I thought that was what the town hall was going to be about – everyone weighing in. I knew that the town was dying and needed this man to pump life back into it. It appeared that everyone agreed that it would be beneficial for the town if they did. If I were a spiteful person, I could have taken the opportunity to destroy Derek's plan to revive the town in one swoop. I didn't know how much what I said to these men would have any bearing on their decision. I realized that I loved this town and the people in it, including Derek, who did everything with the good of the town in mind.

"Okay, well in full disclosure, Mr. Della, I know who you are," I confessed, not wanting him to think that what I said came without an agenda. He nodded and I continued. "The first day I came into town, I remember thinking that from the welcome sign to the bridge, this place looked completely abandoned. Then I got to the bridge and I was so taken aback by the river beneath it that I stopped my car, right on the bridge to admire it. I think that this town is a hidden gem and outsiders would pay good money to spend a weekend here. If the river could become a tourist attraction with rafting and fishing and other excursions the people will come."

"I see you have been privy to the scope of our potential project," Mr. Della said, almost like he was dismissing my opinion because of it.

"It's true I know a little bit about the plan, but before that, I had planned to start my own business here because I saw the potential. Quite honestly, I think the town could fulfill that potential eventually on its own, but if it were to have your backing, it could become what we need it to be now," I said hoping that I sounded confident and not arrogant on my opinion of the town. I held back the nature of my business for one because I wasn't sure if I was legally going to be able to open my B&B and two, because I knew that Mr. Della was planning on building a hotel here.

"That is very insightful," Mr. Della said. "Thank you."

"Of course," I said. "I think your order is up." I walked to the counter to retrieve their breakfast as Dotty gave me a worried look.

Mr. Della and Bill were in deep conversation when I arrived back at their table. This time I was able to gracefully slip their plates in front of them and return to the counter without much disruption. I busied myself behind the counter with anything I could find and wished that someone, anyone would come through the door to order breakfast. Where was everyone today? I kept an eye on the table to make sure I collected their discarded dishes promptly.

"You were right, Holly," Bill said when I came over to remove his plate and refill their coffee. "Those strawberry pancakes were the best things I've ever eaten."

I smiled as I cleared the dishes. "Secretly, those pancakes are the real reason I stayed in town," I teased. They both laughed. At this point, I was hoping to charm them for more than my tip. I felt like the fate of the whole town was riding on my shoulders.

Dotty pulled me aside as I brought the dishes back and told me not to charge them for the meal. I thought that was a nice touch.

I walked back to the table to inform them that their meal was on the house, courtesy of Dotty. They insisted that was not necessary, but they waved thanks to Dotty who was standing in her favorite spot at the front door holding her coffee pot. I thanked them and started to walk back to the front.

"Holly," Mr. Della called after me, "What kind of business are you planning to open?"

Oh no. That was the question that I hoped no one would ask. I answered honestly, "A bed and breakfast."

"This town could use a bed and breakfast," he said.

Chapter Twenty-Four

That night it seemed the whole town was attending the town hall meeting. Everyone that is except me. For better or worse, I already spoke my peace about the town and what it had to offer. I also didn't want to run into Derek. Things with him were just too confusing.

Instead, I planned to stay home, have a glass of wine, and read one of Celia's steamy romance novels, although I couldn't imagine finding a more interesting story in a fiction book than I had in her journals. I was just settling in when there was a knock at the door.

I answered it to find Sam standing in the doorway. I immediately hugged him, hoping he wasn't mad and would reject it. He hugged me back tightly and I invited him in.

"Sam, does your uncle know where you are?" I asked, concerned that he would get in trouble and that Derek might have a panic attack if he found Sam missing one more time.

"He's at the town hall meeting. I was home by myself so it's not like I ran away from another babysitter," he said, like that made it better that he left the house without permission.

"You can't just go out at night by yourself without Derek knowing where you are. He worries," I told him, trying to get the point across finally. "But I'm really glad to see you."

At that, he smiled. I asked him how school was going, and he said it was okay, that some of the kids he friended at the river were in his class and they were nice to him. I told him how happy that made me and started to ask more about it, but he stopped me.

"Holly, I don't want to talk about school," he declared. "I want to talk about the B&B."

"Okay," I said, surprised. "What about it?"

He opened his backpack and pulled out something that looked like it barely fit. Carefully stretching down the sides of the bag as to not break the thing, he finally dislodged it and set it on the counter. It was a scaled model of my house. The detail was amazing – from the white wood front to the black shutters – it was a perfect dollhouse-sized replica. It was smaller than a dollhouse, really, and I had no idea what it was for.

"It's the B&B," he confirmed with a huge grin.

"Yes, it is. It's perfect. Where did you get it?" I asked.

"I made it," he said. "My grandpa helped me."

"Okay, um, is it for me to keep here as decoration?" I guessed.

"No, it is the exact right size to fit in Derek's model of the new town over top of the parking lot he has in this spot instead of the B&B. I measured. I'm going to take it to the town council meeting on Friday and put it in the model," he informed me.

"Oh no, I think that would be a terrible idea," I told him. I couldn't let Derek think Sam had chosen my side over his, worse I didn't want Sam to get in trouble with the town council, the mayor, or his uncle on my behalf.

"What? I thought you would love it. I could just slip it in right before the meeting starts, put it in the model like it has always been there, and then Uncle Derek would have no choice but to say it was part of the original plan or risk looking stupid," he explained, fleshing out the idea.

"Sweetie, I appreciate you wanting to help me, but I can't let you do that," I told him as gently as I could.

"Why not? Don't you want to fight for this?" he asked, sounding much older than his ten-year-old voice allowed. "You know I think the only reason Uncle Derek didn't add it into the model is that he is too scared of what those big investors might think about having some competition about where visitors might decide to stay."

I thought about my conversation earlier with Mr. Della. He didn't seem to be all that worried about my B&B as competition. Maybe we should just pull Derek aside and tell him that. It was a good possibility that he was worried that the B&B would be a deal-breaker for Mr. Della's investment offer. Then maybe he would want to add the B&B into the plan. There she was again, that hopeless romantic, wishing that given the right circumstances and information Derek would choose her on his own. *Be brave. Fight for this.*

"Okay, you're right." I told my tiny co-conspirator, "but we are going to do it my way."

He threw his fist up into the air with a victory "Yes!"

I laughed but told him that I was going to have to do some research first and that I was driving him home immediately before anyone missed him. He reluctantly agreed. The way to his house took us right past the town hall and I could see that I was right, just about the whole town – population 490 - came out for this. I could tell Sam was thinking the same thing because he remarked that he had never seen so many cars parked around the hall.

I dropped Sam off at his house and waited until he was safely inside, locking the door behind him as he promised me. He made me promise to hold onto his backpack with the model he made of the bed and breakfast so that I was sure to have it for whatever I decided to do.

On the way back home, I passed the town hall again. The meeting was still in session. I wondered if all the voices were really being heard inside. I wondered if the whole town agreed that they wanted change and were open to a corporation coming in and buying up some land and changing the town or if there was any dissent about it. The only way I could know for sure was to go into the meeting. So, I found a parking spot on the street with the rest of the cars and walked a block to the town hall.

When I arrived, I quietly slipped in the back, doing my best to draw the least amount of attention I could. Pressing myself up against the back wall, I could see that there was not an empty seat in the house even if I wanted one. Ned was standing at the podium in front of the five town council members and the mayor who sat behind a row of three tables – two to a table, with the mayor and Derek, who was the town council president in the middle.

"I have a few concerns," I heard Ned say, causing chatter in the room. "Don't get me wrong, I want this town to thrive as much as anyone here, but how do we know that all the promises Mr. Della is making are true?" He turned to look at Mr. Della and Bill who were sitting in the front row.

"Ned, that is a valid question," Derek responded. I guess that his role as the president made the meeting his to run.

Before Derek could continue, Mr. Della rose from his seat and said, in a muffled voice as he was not in front of the microphone, "Mr. Sterling, may I address this question?"

Derek nodded and gestured toward the podium. Mr. Della patted Ned's shoulder as Ned moved aside, allowing him in front of the podium. Seeing that the microphone could detach from the podium, he took it out of its holder and moved to the side where he could see the council and the audience as he spoke. "Ned, thank you for asking that question. As Council President Sterling said it is a valid one and one that I am sure many of you are wondering about. I should first tell you that I am a businessman. I have not gotten this far in life and business without taking risks. I am taking a risk by buying property here in a town where at present, there is no reason for people to visit much less need a hotel to stay in. I am not making any promises to you. I am merely investing in your town, but it is up to you to use that money to recreate the town yourselves to attract tourism."

There was loud chatter in the room. It seemed that people were misinformed about what Mr. Della was offering. What I heard, since I arrived, from the townspeople was that some billionaire mogul was coming to purchase the town and rebuild it, not simply buying land and leaving the town to rebuild itself. Thinking about it, when Derek told me about the revitalization plan, he never said that the investor was doing more than just buying land. Apparently, the town rumor mill had gotten it wrong.

"Order! Order!" Derek shouted and pounded his gavel as the townspeople quickly turned on him.

Someone shouted, "That's not what we were told!" and another said, "Why should we just let him buy up land without helping us? And still, another shouted, "We don't need him!"

I have no idea what possessed me, but I moved up through the crowd to the front. Mr. Della saw me and nodded with acknowledgment, remembering me from earlier at the diner. I motioned to him to give me the microphone. Maybe it was divine intervention from Celia who never used her voice and was going to now through me, or maybe I finally decided that I was brave, but regardless of what it was, I tapped the microphone causing it to shriek and quiet and the room.

I thought about what I was wearing, jeans and a t-shirt, appropriate for the night of wine and reading I had planned, but not ideal for speaking in front of a crowd of people. I decided not to think about it and just spoke.

"Good evening," I croaked into the microphone which squeaked again. Adjusting the position of it, I continued. "I'm not sure how many of you know me. I am Holly Jensen. My aunt was Celia Anderson who lived in the old house on Maple Street. I came here leaving behind the city I grew up in to find out that she left the house to me in her will. I stayed because I wanted to turn it into a bed and breakfast. I didn't think twice about it. I've never been one to commit to anything in the past, maybe because I never felt like I was where I was supposed to be – doing what I was supposed to be doing with my life. I never found anything or anyone that made me feel like I belonged. But one look at this town and I wanted to be a part of it, and it embraced me. Dotty with her bottomless coffee pot, Ned and Charlie who came to my aid when I wanted to renovate the house, Sam who gave me purpose every day, and even Derek who has made things interesting. The point is that this town is still on the map because of the people – because of all of you, because of all of us. It is up to us to bring life back to this town and together we can make it happen. Thank you."

I handed the microphone back to Mr. Della and planned to walk back out the way I came in, but the hall erupted with cheers and applause for me. I didn't know what to do. I was frozen where I stood. I looked over at Derek to gauge his reaction. He was on his feet simultaneously clapping, smiling, and shaking his head. I hadn't expected that kind of response from the room or Derek.

The mayor came from around the tables to take the microphone from Mr. Della. He was an intimidating man, not because he was extremely big or tall, he was just the opposite, with a thick black mustache and black hair which was thinning in the back, but he carried himself with authority and spoke sternly. "Thank you, Tony," he said referring to Mr. Della. "And thank you, Holly. We are glad that you are part of this town as well. Especially since you seem to keep Derek on his toes. We can talk about the bulldozer thing another time." He winked at me. I could feel my face redden, but I smiled. I didn't dare look back at Derek.

"Speaking of Derek," the mayor continued, "he has a plan for what we can do to renew this town with the financial help of Tony Della of course. The town council meeting that was scheduled for Friday is going to be held tomorrow instead. It is not open to the public as per usual but by moving the meeting it will allow us to pass along information to everyone sooner. We aren't making it a closed meeting to keep any secrets. I promise you. We just want a chance to work out any details before decisions are made. Please know, as always, we only have the town's best interests in mind." He placed the microphone back on the podium and took his seat back behind the table.

The crowd began to leave the hall, but it bottlenecked at the only two open doors. That meant that I was still stuck in the front of the room. Mr. Della pulled me aside to where he and Bill had been sitting in the front row.

"That was a very moving speech, dear," Mr. Della complimented me.

"Thank you, Mr. Della. I don't know where all that came from. I hadn't planned to say any of it," I confessed.

"Call me Tony, and that just means that you were speaking from the heart. It also means that you are a great motivator and I think your business will be a success. I wonder, would you like to come to the town council meeting tomorrow. Bill and I will be there, and I can tell the mayor that I want you there as my guest. I would like to know your thoughts on what we are bringing to the table," he said.

"I would be honored to be your guest, Tony. Thank you," I said. Suddenly, Sam's plan to fight for my B&B didn't seem so impossible after all.

Chapter Twenty-Five

I called my parents the next day because I hadn't checked in with them since they returned home from the weekend they spent at the house. I was sure they were wondering how things were going with Derek and me. It was nice that they weren't hounding me about it but were letting me handle things on my own.

"Hi Mom," I said when she picked up the phone.

"Holly! Hon, it's Holly," she yelled to my dad, obviously trying to muffle herself with her hand over the phone which translated on my end to crackling and yelling. "Sweetie, how are you?"

"I'm doing okay," I told her.

"Holly!" my dad said into the other extension. I think that my parents may be the last people to have a landline these days, but it came in handy because then I could talk to them both at the same time.

"Hi Dad," I said, happy to hear both of their voices. "How are you guys?"

"Oh, you know, same old same old," my dad answered. "How is the bed and breakfast?"

"How are things with Derek?" my mom chimed in.

"Well, I finally told Derek about the deed being in his grandfather's name only. He didn't take it very well. Rightly so, and we haven't had much contact since. The thing is that I read in one of Celia's diaries that she and Graham were secretly married before he died so that would mean that the house was really hers and thus really mine, but I haven't told Derek that part yet," I blurted, not even pausing to breath.

There was silence on the other end of the phone which I took to mean they were trying to figure out what to say. Finally, my dad broke the silence. "Okay, so has Derek asked you to leave the house?"

That seemed like a strange take away from all I had just recounted, but in truth that could be a possibility. As my dad, he held my safety and well-being as his first concern I concluded. "Well, no, he hasn't. We haven't talked about it at all," I answered.

"What about that lawyer guy? Did you tell him that you thought Celia was married to Derek's grandfather at the time of his death?" my dad asked, coming up with something else I hadn't done.

"His name is Randy. No, I meant to call him and then something came up with Sam and I never did," I answered. I was starting to feel like a child that hadn't thought anything through. I was coming down off the buzz from last night's speech to the town very quickly now.

"Holly, do you want this bed and breakfast to work or is this just another thing you thought you would try and then abandon?" my mom chimed in unapologetically.

Ouch.

"Well, that was harsh, but you're right. I have a history of not following through with things, but this time is different. I will make this bed and breakfast a reality. I think I just want it all – the house, the dream job, the guy, the family," I said, realizing that truth for the first time as the words came out of my mouth.

"Honey, sometimes you can't have it all," my dad said, glumly. "You can only control yourself and how you react. If you want this bed and breakfast, you are going to have to fight for it."

"Thanks Dad. I'll make a call first thing tomorrow. I'm not that girl anymore Mom, I know what I want and I'm brave enough to go for it."

I finished my conversation with them, promising to keep them updated and ask them for help if I needed it.

I needed to get ready for the meeting tonight. What do you wear to a town planning meeting when the man you love is planning to tear down your potential business to make a parking lot because he thinks he owns the land, but you have told the biggest investor your plan for opening that business and he thinks you are so insightful he invited you to the meeting all the while not knowing anything about anything and you have to speak in front of the scary mayor? *A power suit. You wear a power suit.*

I have interviewed so many times that I invested in a nice business suit. The black hip length tailored jacket had one button at the waist and underneath, I wore a silky white camisole. The black pants were fitted to my ankle and I wore black kitten heels to pull it all together. That suit gave me confidence every time I wore it and I never needed more confidence than I did today. I let my long red hair flow down my back and kept my makeup neutral except for bold red lipstick.

I gave myself a quick once over in the mirror. I was impressed with what I saw. I hoped the town council, the mayor, Mr. Della, and Derek would be impressed too – not just with how I looked, but the whole package. *No pressure*, I thought sarcastically to myself.

I still had Sam's backpack with the model of the B&B inside sitting in my car. I went over so many scenarios in my head. In one, the model of the town was sitting in the middle of the room and everyone was circling around to see it. While Derek was explaining all the changes, I would swiftly pull out the model B&B and place it over the parking lot space and say, "The town isn't complete without this." Or, "Derek I think you left this behind in your office." Then he would be compelled to leave it in the plan or look like a fool. In another scenario, as everyone looked over the town model, Mr. Della would say "Holly, where is your bed & breakfast in this?" and I would either wait for Derek to explain or save him by handing him the scaled B&B like he had just forgotten to add it. I hadn't perfected my approach, but I wasn't sure that any of those ideas would go over very well.

By the time I had played and replayed as many scenarios in my head as I could think of, I was at the Town Hall, ten minutes early. I parked on the street and took a deep breath trying to calm myself. I had a moment of panic when I looked down at my sharp suit and worried that maybe they didn't dress up for these meetings. Maybe since it was a closed meeting, and this was a small town everyone wore casual clothes like it was casual Friday or something. No matter. I was going in wearing my tailored suit and I would own it.

I got out of the car and grabbed Sam's backpack, which didn't go well with my outfit. I shut the door and walked the few feet to the town hall. I hoped the door would be open since I was a little early. To my relief it was. Like I imagined in several of my scenarios of how this meeting would go, the scaled model of the town was in the middle of the room on top of two tables that were pushed together to support it. At least that's what I assumed was in the middle of the room because it was completely covered up with black fabric indicating there would be a big reveal. I wondered if anyone else besides me had seen it because I only saw it by accident.

Derek was early too. Probably there to set up the display. Thankfully, he too was wearing a suit and I felt like I had chosen properly after all. He was pacing around the room reviewing notecards and stopped when he saw me. He was nervous. It hadn't occurred to me that he would be. He always seemed to be confident and in control of every situation. Seeing him nervous drove home just how big a deal this meeting was for the town. I started to wonder if my plan about adding the homemade model of the B&B to the town display was a good one. Was I being selfish in only thinking of my part in this? I had this great idea that running a bed and breakfast in a little town would be something out of a romance novel. My practical side knew that the town needed to change and grow to survive and that a plan needed to be in place to help the whole town, not just my burgeoning business. That was the reason I was there, not to make a scene that would only be self-serving. I was following the idea of a ten-year-old boy and it was childish. I removed the backpack from my shoulder and tucked it under a chair.

Derek walked over to me and smiled weakly. "Hi," he said softly. "I'm glad you're here early. I thought maybe we could talk."

He wasn't surprised to see me, so I guessed that Tony had told everyone that I was coming. That was a relief to me. Worrying about being overdressed was more about not being a welcome participant in the meeting and feeling like maybe I had no business being there at all. I still hoped that was not the case.

"Okay," I answered, and I met him where he was standing in front of the tables that held the model of the town, still covered up.

"I'm sorry for everything – for trying to bully you into giving up the house with the bulldozers and the letter. I'm sorry for not speaking to you the last few weeks. I was angry that you didn't show me the deed sooner because if you had we wouldn't have spent so much time getting to know each other and my decision about what to do with the house would have been simple. I felt like I had to choose between the town and you. The thing is ..." He trailed off as the door to the hall creaked open and Tony and Bill came in followed by the mayor and the rest of the town council.

"Derek and Holly," Tony said, coming in with open arms toward us. He stopped to shake Derek's hand and pat the top of his arm. When he got to me, he shook my hand too. He was a genuinely nice guy.

"Tony," Derek said, disengaging completely from the conversation with me. "I am so glad you could come."

"I'm not sure I introduced you to my friend Bill," Tony said, pulling Bill into our circle. "This is Bill Winston. He might be interested in making an investment in the town as well."

"It's nice to meet you. I want to see the plans first before I make any offers, but I like what I have seen so far," Bill said, shaking Derek's hand. "Holly, I went back to the diner again this morning. I can't get enough of those strawberry pancakes," he said switching from shaking Derek's hand to mine.

"I told you they were the best thing on the menu," I said, smiling. I noticed the look of confusion on Derek's face or maybe it was the increasing pressure of the day that made his eyes squint and his brow furrow.

The mayor stepped into our group to welcome Tony and Bill and greet Derek. When he got to me, he said, "Holly, thank you for coming. I think it was a great idea to have your input as someone who has a stake in the town, but also an outsider's view to bring fresh perspective. Most of us have lived here our whole lives and might not see changes the way we should."

With the sincere welcome from the mayor and my role here at the meeting finally defined, I felt myself relax a bit and I took a seat at one of the tables encircling the display. I looked around the room at the other council members. There were three men and a woman. I recognized Greg McFarland from the market as one member. The pharmacist who I had seen coming and going from the doctor's office/pharmacy that was across the street from my house was another. He introduced himself as Bob Long. The final male member of the council was introduced as Ken Straub, the owner of the pub at the end of town that I hadn't made my way to as I thought I might on my first day here. The sole female member of the council, I discovered was Penny White, an attorney who worked at Randy's firm. Everyone had taken their seats except for Derek who was standing in the middle of the circle of tables with the display behind him. This was his show after all.

"Thank you all for coming today," Derek said and then paused to bend down to get something beneath the covered display table. He stood and brought up eight binders from under the table. He passed one out to each of us. Skimming through it, I saw that it was a fifty-page proposal on how to revitalize the town. I was beyond impressed with all the work that must have gone into creating this document. "In these binders you will find a plan for how to bring life back to this town. The land where Tony has agreed to purchase and build one of his lodges is owned by the town and so the money goes back into the town and will be used to create business and tourism. You can read more specifics in the proposal, but I wanted to give a summary of what we can do to stimulate our economy."

Tony stood, interrupting Derek. "Before Derek goes further in his plan, I want full disclosure on my purchase of the property. I am not in the business of losing money. That said, I am willing to take a risk and build in your town because I think it has potential. However, once I purchase the property, it is mine to resell to whomever I want if my hotel is not thriving. I have agreed to a three-year contract to keep the property, but after that amount of time, if it is losing money it is within my right to sell it." Tony sat and returned the floor to Derek.

"Thank you for your honesty Tony," Derek said sincerely. "So that is the time frame we are working with. But here is how we are going to do it."

Derek went on to talk about offering microgrants to townspeople who want to start new businesses like Dotty who, besides the diner, has always wanted to open a bakery. He stressed the idea that the vacant buildings needed to be used. He proposed a co-op where the residents of the town would put their money into new ventures like a river adventure excursion business so that they would have a stake in its success. His ideas were brilliant with out-of-the-box thinking and you could feel the excitement they brought to the room.

The mayor stood to address the council. "Ladies and gentlemen, it is important that we get your input and your vote regarding the sale of the town's property to Mr. Tony Della. I know you all need time to read the large document provided, but let's please go around the room and give your preliminary thoughts on this plan. We will have a final vote next week."

Penny White was the first to speak. She was probably in her late forties and wore a suit, much like mine but with a pencil shirt instead of pants. As an attorney, she wanted to make sure all legal bascs had been covered. "If we start a tourism co-op which promotes white water rafting or fishing on the river and someone gets hurt or God forbid dies, they or their loved ones could sue the town and bankrupt it. Is there a plan in place for that unfortunate circumstance?"

"The town will have an insurance policy in place as well as having participants sign waivers. There are more details in the document," Derek answered confidently.

Penny nodded, satisfied with his answer. Greg McFarland spoke next. "My family has run the grocery store for generations. If we let a hotel chain purchase land in town, will it stop there, or will I have to worry about a Walmart popping up next and stealing all my business?"

"We aren't interested in commercializing the town," the mayor said, fielding this question. "Part of the appeal for tourists is the small-town charm and a relaxing getaway. We don't need big box stores to clutter our glorious landscape. If people want to go to Walmart they will have to stop there before they leave home."

The other council members voiced their concerns and Derek and the mayor addressed them to satisfaction it seemed. Then it was my turn to talk.

"Holly Jensen is here with us tonight as a guest of Mr. Della's. She is a new resident with aspirations of building a business here and we thought that her take on our plan would be useful," the mayor said, explaining my presence.

The way he introduced me made me realize that I was here on behalf of the hotel chain and my part was to sell the idea to the council. Thankfully, I was onboard with the plan and I didn't have to stretch very far to express that.

"This town is charming," I began, "and I was given an opportunity to start a business here which I decided to take based on the town's charm alone, but when I stopped to think more deeply about it I had to ask myself if that was a good decision. Like Mr. Della, but on a much, much smaller scale, I could have taken my money and started a business anywhere. Looking around at the town and how small it really is and how outsiders don't have a reason to stop here or to plan a getaway here, I really thought that I was making a bad decision by staying. When I got wind of the town being revitalized and after meeting so many members of this community who I knew would do what it takes to make that happen, I felt confident that my decision was the right one."

I looked over at Derek to see him smiling at me. Everyone seemed to take in what I said and think about their decisions as business owners to remain in the town. It was in the best interest of everyone to let this happen.

"Thank you everyone for your feedback. Finally, I want to show you what our town could look like if we work together to make it successful." With that he carefully pulled the black cloth off the model of the town. Everyone got up from their seats to get a better look at it.

I hung back a little. After all I had already had a sneak peek of it. Listening to the others talk about it was like being at a train garden at Christmas. "Look there's Dotty's Diner," and "The trees look so real," and "The little bus even has the name of the white water rafting company on it." The other thing that made me think of people at a train garden was the pure joy it brought to them.

"Holly," Tony said, coming back to find me, "take a look." He pulled me forward so I could get a better look. I took a deep breath and walked up to it with him, dreading the thought of seeing the parking lot where my house used to be, and hoping that he wouldn't ask me where my bed and breakfast was.

I didn't raise my eyes until I was right in front of it. Of course, in an act of self-torture I sought out the vacant spot that used to be the beautiful old house. To my surprise, it was there – a perfect replica of my house including a tiny sign that read "Sterling Manor Bed and

Breakfast." I gasped and immediately looked for Derek who I found across the table watching me for my reaction.

The room started to clear after a few minutes with council members shaking Derek's hand and the mayor patting him on the back for a job well done. Soon the only people remaining were Derek, Tony, Bill, and me. I wanted the other two to leave so badly so that I could talk to Derek alone.

"Derek," Bill called, getting his attention. "Tony brought me here because my company franchises businesses for tourism like white water rafting tours or zipline adventures. I would very much be interested in starting a franchise here. Between the townspeople who might want to partake in your co-op idea and my team who specializes in getting the business up and running, I think we could be extremely successful."

"That would be amazing," Derek said. This was like the icing on the cake after his successful pitch to the council. He was beaming.

The two shook hands and then Bill turned to me. "Holly, if I am being honest you are the real reason I came here," Bill said out of nowhere.

I just stared at him for a moment before asking, "The reason for coming to the meeting?" I had absolutely no idea where he was going with this.

"No, you are the reason I came to the town," he said cryptically. Now I was confused. How did he even know who I was before he met me at the diner?

"I am sorry. I don't understand," I told him honestly.

"My mother, as it turns out, was a childhood friend of your Aunt Celia. They kept in touch over the years, so I knew about this little town of Friendsville. In fact, she was a nanny for a family and lived here for a little while herself," he explained.

Emma. His mother was Emma, the girl who introduced Celia to Graham. He had no idea that Derek was the son of one of the children she cared for when she was a nanny. Just when I thought Celia's spirit had gone to rest, she brings Bill here. I no longer believed in coincidences.

"Oh, it is such a small world," I replied. I thought of asking his mother's name to confirm my hunch, but I really didn't need to.

"When Tony told me about the opportunity, I thought maybe it was divine intervention," he said. I stifled a laugh. "I told my mother that I was visiting her old town this week and she said that Celia had family here and told me I should give them this." He pulled out an envelope and handed it to me. He didn't wait around to watch me open it, but instead collected Tony and they both said their goodbyes to Derek.

I held the envelope wondering what could be in it, but knew it was for meant for me because Celia didn't have family in Friendsville. I carefully opened it to find a page from a journal that Celia had written not long before she died. It was not addressed to me, but the words on the page spoke to me directly.

January 1, 2018

"If I loved you less, I might be able to talk about it more."

Jane Austen, Emma

It has been nearly sixty-five years since I kept a diary – journaled, as it is called now. I didn't want to talk to anyone, not even myself. I thought if I let out my feelings, they would crush me. So instead, I lived a lifetime in a house, that was not mine alone with my sorrow. I never let anyone in. Not into my heart and rarely into the house. I was once a young girl full of life and hope for the future until reality crashed into my dream, killing it instantly.

I tried to freeze time to never change anything from when I was the happiest, but time does not freeze. It moves on with or without you. If you do not change with the time, you wither away like the paint on a wall, peeling and cracking and becoming something ugly, something old and broken.

You can be brave and live life to the fullest, overcoming all obstacles, or you can let life wear you down until you are a mere survivor of its cruelness. It is your choice.

Had I the chance to live it again, I would still choose love. But I fear we do not get second chances when time runs out and my time here has come to its end.

Tears came to my eyes as I read it. She was telling me to be brave and not run away from love even if it hurt. I felt Derek come up beside me and put his arm around me. He didn't speak. He was just there. The envelope held one more thing – a photograph of Celia at seventeen. She was stunningly beautiful with wide, carefree eyes and a gleaming smile with high cheek bones. The photo was in black and white, but I imagined that her hair was red, like mine.

Derek looked over my shoulder at the photo. "She was beautiful. No wonder my grandfather was in love with her," he said and looked at me. "You look just like her in this picture."

I smiled. "Sterling Manor, huh?" I asked, moving on to the matter at hand.

"I thought Celia would like that name," he said, stepping back and winking.

"Since it is your house, I guess you will be opening a bed and breakfast?" I asked, taunting him a little.

"What I was trying to tell you before was that I felt like I had to choose between you and the town. I chose you. Then I realized that you are good for this town," he confessed, moving a little closer to me. "And for me too."

"Oh really? Did the ghost of a relative past pay you a visit to tell you that?" I asked, still teasing, but moving toward him to close the gap between us.

He laughed. "No, actually it was a feisty waitress with a crystal ball that looked a lot like a coffee pot who told me that." I laughed. *Oh, sweet Dotty and her relentless meddling.* "I am willing to let you go half on the bed and breakfast, by the way," he continued, "You should probably have someone witness that I just offered you that deal."

"Looks like you and I are the only ones here," I said, referring to the empty hall and that there was no sign of Celia or Graham.

"Do you think they're gone?" Derek asked. I knew exactly which "they" he was referring to.

"I think getting the two of us together was their unfinished business," I answered.

He smiled and took me in his arms. "Well we better make sure they know they can rest in peace now." He leaned down and he kissed me to seal the deal.

Epilogue

July 18, 2019

Ever since I read Celia's journals, I have wanted to start journaling myself. Who knows maybe someday my grandchildren will want to read the story of my life? Since I've only just started today, I might have to go back and fill in some blanks for them as to how I got here to this moment that I am writing about, but for now, I will start right where I am.

A lot happened in the year and a half since that day I rode into Friendsville with basically everything I owned in the world stuffed into my tiny car and was yelled at by a stranger in a diner.

The town council unanimously voted to let the sale of the town's property go through and it became the home of The Della Hotel, a thirty-room lodge at the edge of town that offered guests a place to sleep, a continental breakfast, and a pool. With the creation of Troubled River Tours, thanks to Bill Winston, which offered white water rafting and tubing, as well as McFarland Charters, a secret passion of Greg's who was an avid fisherman, that offered fishing charters for individuals and small groups looking for a fishing excursion, the town had plenty of attractions.

We started a huge marketing campaign introducing the world to our little town – the hidden gem of Friendsville where a weekend getaway was just a short drive from the city. My dad passed out business cards as he promised as well and from that, we got an annual commitment from his company for a staff retreat. It turned out that Penny White's sister was the founder of a well-known wedding website that graciously toted Friendsville as the place to get married if you wanted a wedding in the woods and a honeymoon on the river. We created a town website and promoted it on social media. While it was going to take the full three years to turn the town into a thriving vacation spot, we were well on our way.

Sterling Manor Bed and Breakfast has become *the* place for wedding parties to stay, bachelorette weekends, and anniversary celebrations thanks to Penny's sister. My favorite bachelorette party to date was that of my former roommate, Darla who coincidentally spent her bachelorette weekend here. She finally landed the man of her dreams with a six-carat diamond on her finger to prove it. Perry was also among Darla's guests, reluctant as she might have been. I went all out for that party to make sure it was a blast with maybe a little extra *in your face* thrown it there.

Sam and I have become quite a force in my dream kitchen. Together we whip up new menu ideas weekly. We've made muffins, blueberry bread, tater tot bakes, quiche – anything that we can think of together . He is always available as my taste tester and I love being able to spend so much time with him.

We have all five bedrooms filled most of the time. There were a lot of happy couples and soon-to-be couples who stayed there. I think that would be exactly what Celia would have wanted. I finally told Derek that Celia and Graham had gotten married and that Celia was officially a Sterling. He took that opportunity to ask if I wanted to become a Sterling too. I am pretty sure his proposal was better than that, but I was too overwhelmed with joy to remember it exactly.

Derek and I got married on New Year's Eve in front of our friends and family just like Celia and Graham had hoped to do. My parents were almost as happy as Sam was at the wedding. We were finally and officially a family. Our newest addition to the family, a girl, is due to arrive in two months. We decided to name her Vivien Celia Sterling.

Ned and his guys finally turned the garage in the back of the bed and breakfast into the innkeepers' quarters. Derek sold his house and bought the property behind the B&B, so my dream cottage turned into a proper house – not as big as the B&B, but plenty of room for all of us to live comfortably.

I love being a wife, a mother, and owner of a bed and breakfast. I have truly found my calling, finally after a long search. I am fully committed to all my roles. If I hadn't tried all the things I did to find my way before I got to this place, who knows if I would have gotten here at all.

Celia showed me how wonderful love could feel and exactly where to find it. And when I worry that I am not enough, she whispers in my ear, "Be brave," and I know that I can take on the world.

Dotty's Famous Strawberry Pancakes

INGREDIENTS

2 cups all-purpose flour
¼ cup granulated sugar
½ teaspoon salt
1 teaspoon baking powder
½ teaspoon baking soda

2 cups buttermilk
2 large eggs
4 tablespoons vegetable oil
1½ cups sliced strawberries
Strawberry Sauce for serving
Strawberry Jam for serving
Butter for serving

INSTRUCTIONS

In a large mixing bowl, whisk together flour, sugar, salt, baking powder, and baking soda and set aside.

In a small bowl, whisk together the buttermilk, eggs, and oil.

Create a well in the center of the dry ingredients and add the wet ingredients and 1 cup of the sliced strawberries, mixing with a rubber spatula just until combined. The batter will be lumpy. Do not to overbeat the batter.

Place the batter in the refrigerator for 20 minutes until bubbles start to form all over the top.

Preheat the oven or your warming drawer to 200°F and line a baking sheet with parchment paper. This will be used to put any cooked pancakes on so they don't get cold and soggy while you're cooking up the rest of the batter.

Heat a griddle to 350°F or a large skillet over medium heat and spray with nonstick spray.

Add ¼ cup of the pancake batter to the griddle or pan to make each pancake. Add a few additional slices of strawberries to the pancakes.

Once the tops are all bubbly and the bottoms are golden brown, flip the pancakes and cook until done. Repeat until the batter is gone.

SERVING

Stack two pancakes on a plate and cover with strawberry sauce and a slice of butter. Stack two more on top of those and repeat. Add the final two pancakes.Top with strawberry jam, a slice of butter and 2-3 fresh strawberries on the very top. Never skimp on the presentation.

**Remember: Always have your coffee pot ready
and pour with a smile!**

Bio

I'm Jenn (two n's, please). I was raised in Perry Hall, Maryland where I wrote my first book, *The Adventures of Freddie Field Mouse* at age 7. It got critical acclaim from my parents, grandparents and many aunts and uncles.

Unfortunately, the original manuscript was lost or may be still under my childhood bed (sorry Mom, I will clean that out someday).

I continued writing novels through high school, but turned my focus to graphic design as a career.

My first job out of college was as a graphic designer for a newspaper. I later co-published a local newspaper where I was a contributing writer and graphic designer. Later I joined a well-known newspaper as the Art Director and freelanced as a columnist for an online newspaper.

In 2013, I became the Marketing Production Supervisor for a large library system where I am surrounded by books all the time.

I still live in Baltimore, Maryland with my husband, five-year-old son and two cats. You can find me listening to audiobooks or writing in between juggling my full-time job and managing virtual kindergarten.

Acknowledgments

There are so many people who helped and supported me with this book. My family and friends were the first to cheer me on when I decided to self-publish this novel. I was also embraced by the writing community on social media. Together we can support each other and make our dreams come true.

I would like to thank my editor and best friend, Beth Suit for starting on this writing journey with me back in 2006 when I asked her to read a manuscript I had written. Actually, way before that she might have been my first beta reader all the way back in middle school. She's the one who was immediately all in when I told her I wanted to publish this novel.

To my husband...thank you for hearing my idea about publishing a book, telling me to go for it and giving me the space to make it happen.

To my Logan...thank you for being my sunshine and always going to bed on time so I was able to write.

To my family, especially my mom, who has always been my greatest cheering section.

I have found the best beta readers ever who helped me craft this debut novel into more than I realized it could be. To Roxana for editing my lines and forgiving the times when I write like Yoda.

The Legacy of Sterling Manor has been such a joy to write and a dream come true. I hope you enjoyed it!

CPSIA information can be obtained
at www.ICGtesting.com
Printed in the USA
LVHW021511150621
690286LV00002B/328